MY FIVE DATES

A LOVE LIKE THAT NOVEL

R.L. KENDERSON

ISBN-13: 978-1-950918-32-4

Editor: Jovana Shirley, Unforeseen Editing, www.unforeseenediting.com
Cover image:
Photographer: Wander Aguiar, Wander Book Club, www.wanderbook-club.com
Model: Zack Salaun
Designer: R.L. Kenderson at R.L. Cover Designs, www.rlcoverdesigns.com

MY FIVE DATES

PROLOGUE

SLOAN

I WATCHED my best friend throw herself down on my couch, head practically in my lap, in a fit of tears.

"Why? Why did he have to do that? Why do men have to be such dogs?"

I rubbed Melanie's back. "I don't know, honey. Because men suck?"

She looked up at me, her brown eyes watery. "They *do* suck. You got that right."

She slammed her blonde head back down, and Bear, my Newfoundland-mix dog, put his big brown head on Melanie's back.

"I'm sorry he cheated on you," I told her because I really was.

Neil Stanton and I weren't fans of each other, but I would never want my friend to get hurt.

Melanie had just come over after her dumbass boyfriend had accidentally synced his iPhone to her iPad, letting Melanie read every one of the sexy text messages he'd

1

exchanged with someone who wasn't Melanie. It was the same iPad he'd given her for her birthday because he'd been late to meet her for dinner and felt guilty. He'd probably been boning his side chick. Oh, the irony.

"I hate men."

"Me, too, Mel," I said in solidarity.

She looked up at me again. "Yeah, but you hate men for no real reason. I hate men because they're cheaters."

I looked away and rolled my eyes. "Fine, then I don't hate men."

Mel's lower lip wobbled. "But you just told me you hated them."

I sighed and rubbed her back again. "Yes, I hate them. Just for you, Mel."

She laid her head back down and sniffled. "Thank you."

After Melanie could cry no more tears, I helped her to the guest room and tucked her in like she was a child and I was her parent.

The next morning, I was sitting at my kitchen table, drinking coffee and scrolling through social media, when Melanie came out, rubbing her eyes.

"Hey, hon. How are you doing?" I asked.

Melanie plopped down in the chair adjacent to me and held up her phone. "He didn't even ask what happened to me last night. I was supposed to go to his house."

I turned off the screen of my phone and set it down. I propped my arms on the table and leaned in close. "So … what do you want us to do about it?"

Her eyes narrowed. "I want to fucking get even."

I grinned like the Cheshire cat and practically rubbed my hands together. "Let's do it."

I couldn't wait. Nobody walked all over Sloan Zehler's friends and got away with it.

ONE

CALEB

"THANK YOU, SIR," I said to my final customer of the day and breathed a sigh of relief when he walked out the door.

I'd spent almost an hour with him, and he hadn't bought a single thing. I didn't work on commission, but it was still frustrating.

I looked around the used sporting goods store. I wanted this place to thrive, for more reasons than one, and it wasn't going to happen when people continually came in and didn't buy anything.

"It's five, guys. I'm done for the day," I told the three staff members on the floor.

"Okay," one of them said without looking my way.

Yeah, they were going to miss me.

I walked back to the break room to grab my stuff before I headed home.

My phone buzzed. It was my mother.

Mom: Don't forget about dinner tonight, sweetie.

I groaned. I loved my family, but I had been looking forward to doing my own thing tonight.

> Me: I'll be there. Just getting off work now.

I grabbed my wallet and keys from my locker and headed for the door, but I stopped when I saw my boss—the owner of the shop—sitting at his desk in his office. I'd been wanting to speak to him all week, but he hadn't been around much.

I knocked on the open door.

Ted Goldman looked up from his paperwork and smiled at me. Unfortunately, it was strained, which didn't bode well for what I wanted to speak to him about.

"Hey, Caleb. Can I help you with something?"

I walked into the office and took the chair right across from him. "I wanted to know if you'd considered my offer."

Ted was almost in his seventies now and getting ready to retire. His wife had done so the year before, and the two of them wanted to do some traveling. While Ted had some good managers running his store, it was still a full-time job, and he was looking to sell.

And I was looking to buy.

I was one of the good managers Ted had on staff—correction, I was a great manager. I'd been working at the store since I was sixteen, minus one year back when I was twenty, making my total years of employment fourteen.

I had the most seniority *and* loyalty, and Ted was like a second father to me. I figured I was his first choice. In fact, I figured I wouldn't even have any competition, but the look on Ted's face said I wasn't going to like what he had to say.

Ted set his pen down and sighed. "I have thought about it, but I'm going to have to say no."

"No?" *No?* I'd thought he'd at least counter my offer. A flat-out no wasn't something I'd even considered. "Did you change your mind about selling?"

A look of regret filled Ted's face. "No. I'm going to sell it to Rick."

"*What?*" I said as I flew to my feet. "*Rick?*"

"Shh," Ted said. "Close the door."

I did as he'd requested because I didn't want people listening in on our conversation any more than Ted did.

I crossed my arms over my chest. "Rick has only been here a year and a half. He's not even full-time," I argued.

Rick was Ted's nephew and had only started working here after his wife and kids left him. He was trying to make extra money to pay for his lawyer and child support.

"I know, Caleb. But, if I sell the place to Rick, he can work here full-time and spend more time with his kids because he won't be working two jobs."

"This is fucking nepotism."

Ted's chair screeched as he pushed it back and rose to his feet. "You will not swear at me, young man. And this is not nepotism."

I held out my arms. "Young man? Ted, I'm thirty-one years old. I have been here since I was sixteen. I've been a manager for nine years. You explain to me why this isn't nepotism, and I won't fight you."

Ted rubbed his hand over his eyes and sat down. "I started this store back in the late eighties. I'm the only one who's ever owned it. It's my baby. And I can't just leave it to someone …"

I sat down again. "Someone what?"

"Someone who might sell it in a few years."

I frowned. "Why the hell do you think I would do that?"

"You have nothing tying you down, Caleb. You rent your apartment, you're not married, and you don't have any kids. Plus, you don't have the best track record."

"Excuse me?"

"You quit college. You almost signed up for the military but decided at the last minute to go backpacking through Europe for a year."

"That was over ten years ago," I protested.

"I realize that, but I still don't know that you're not going to decide to do something like that again. Maybe ten years is your tipping point. And, like I said, you have nothing tying you down."

"I have my family," I pointed out.

"They didn't stop you from leaving them the last time. Meanwhile, Rick has a mortgage, child support, and children keeping him around. He's not going anywhere." Ted folded his arms on his desk. "Look, you are both excellent workers. You know you've done a lot for this store. *I* know you've done a lot. But I have to look at this objectively."

I wasn't ready to give up yet, and a plan was forming in my brain. "Have you told Rick this yet?"

"No."

Yes! I exclaimed inside my head.

"Why?" Ted asked as if he almost wanted me to have another reason.

There was still hope.

"Because what if I told you that I'd been looking for

houses and that there was actually a special woman in my life?"

Ted sat back in his chair and narrowed his eyes. "I'd ask why you never said anything. You always tell us about your girlfriends." He crossed his arms. "And why wouldn't you have mentioned house-hunting?"

Think fast, Caleb.

"I didn't mention the house-hunting because I didn't want it to influence your decision on selling the store. I see now that it was a mistake."

Damn. I was so impressed with that lie that I was mentally patting myself on the back.

Ted's arms fell. He believed me. "And the girl?"

"Woman, I corrected." I looked down at my feet like I was embarrassed. "I really like her." I looked up at Ted. "Don't laugh, but I think this one might be special."

"Hmm ..." That was an *I'm not sure I believe you quite yet* hmm.

"You know I've never said that about anyone before." I might talk about the women I'd dated, but I'd never said any of them were special.

"This is true." He studied me, and I could tell he still didn't quite trust me. "What's her name?"

My phone started playing my special ringtone for my mother.

Saved by the fucking bell.

I held up my finger to Ted and answered my cell, "Hello?"

"Caleb, I need you to pick something up on your way here."

9

"Okay. Hold on one second, Mom." I pulled the receiver away from my mouth and stood. "Sorry, Ted, I have to go. Please, can we continue this conversation later?" I begged him with my eyes to reconsider.

"Fine."

I grinned. "Thank you." I turned and walked out the door. "Mom, I'm back. What did you need?"

"But, Caleb?" Ted said.

"Hold on again, Mom." I spun back around outside the door. "Yes?"

"Bring her to dinner tomorrow night."

"Who?"

Ted's eyebrows jumped to his hairline. "Your girlfriend."

Oh shit. I laughed nervously. "Yeah, okay." I pointed to my phone. "For a second there, I thought you were talking about my mom." *Awesome save, Caleb.*

Ted shook his head. "Get out of here. I'll see you tomorrow night."

"Okay." I spun again and bolted away before he could say anything else. "Mom, you still there?"

"I'm here. Did I interrupt anything important?" she asked.

Just my future. "Nothing that can't wait."

"Oh, good. Can you pick up an extra package of hamburger buns on your way here?"

I hurried out of the store before Ted. "Sure. Not a problem."

"Thank you. See you soon then?"

"Yep. I'll be there soon."

I hung up my phone and unlocked my car.

My to-do list was now buying hamburger buns, finding a realtor, and convincing someone to play my girlfriend. All by tomorrow night. I suddenly had an extremely busy weekend.

TWO
SLOAN

MELANIE and I decided that the best revenge against Neil was to go after the thing he loved most in the world. His 1969 Chevrolet Camaro.

Unfortunately, that was easier said than done.

Neil never left his car parked outside, and Mel and I both decided that it would look too suspicious if someone broke into his garage and vandalized his car.

Our next option was work, but his employer's parking lot had cameras in it.

We considered doing the job when he was at Melanie's place, but we thought it might point the finger at us. Plus, half the time, he asked to park in the extra stall in her garage. It would seem suspicious if she told him no and then his car turned up, ruined.

We might be conniving, but we weren't stupid.

Also, Mel and I decided that we had to be around to see Neil's reaction. It wouldn't be any fun if we only got to hear about it. That was why Melanie hadn't broken up with Neil yet. That, and she'd be the number one suspect if they'd recently broken up.

Finally, the perfect opportunity came up. Almost perfect. Neil's parents were having a family dinner. It still had some risks, but a better opportunity wasn't coming along. They usually lasted at least a couple of hours, and as long as no one walked outside, we'd be fine.

Our plan was for me to drop Melanie off for dinner, and I was going to pick her up later for a ladies' night, which was when the car would be discovered. It was going to be great.

"What time is it?" I asked, holding the binoculars up to my eyes.

"Almost five thirty," Mel said.

I lowered my hands. "Are you sure Caleb is coming?"

"Yes."

"What is taking him so long?" I asked, not expecting an answer. "If I don't drop you off by six, Neil is going to wonder what's up."

"Are you sure? I feel like he hasn't given a shit about me lately."

I put my hand on Mel's arm. "I'm sorry, honey. But remember that feeling you have right now when we're coating his car with brake fluid."

I had Googled ways to ruin car paint—at the library, thank you very much—and there were a lot of options. I'd really wanted to go with some strong paint remover, but Melanie had thought it was too harsh. The asshole deserved harsh, but it wasn't worth it if it was going to stress my friend out.

Just when I thought I couldn't handle the anticipation anymore, Caleb's black Toyota Tundra pulled up. Personally, I thought a man driving a truck was sexier than driving a classic car, but I didn't say that out loud.

I pulled the binoculars up to my face again and watched the back of Caleb's tawny head as he walked into the house.

"Okay, he's inside. Let's give him five minutes to make sure he didn't forget anything, and then it's game on."

We waited ten minutes because Mel was getting nervous before getting out of my dad's truck. I wasn't dumb enough to park my own car down the street from the Stantons' home.

It also helped that my father worked as a landscaper. Having his work truck parked outside with various things like shovels looked more natural. To complete the look, we wore shorts and T-shirts and baseball caps with the company logo.

I grabbed the two bottles of brake fluid from the back and handed one to Mel.

"I still can't believe brake fluid is bad."

"It's not that bad. It'll just leave streaks in his paint job." At least, that was what I'd gotten from the YouTube videos I'd watched.

She bit her lip.

"Mel, come on. He can afford to spend a thousand bucks on a paint job. Think of everything he's put you through."

Her eyes narrowed. "You're right. I'm just struggling with the angel on my shoulder, who is telling me this is wrong."

Funny. I had no trouble telling my angel to shut up.

I put my hand on her shoulder. "This won't ruin his car in any way. He'll still be able to drive it. He'll still be safe. It's not like we're cutting his brake line or anything." I tapped my chin. "Although …"

Mel playfully shoved me. "Hey now. No murder."

I laughed. "You're right." Even I had my limits.

I reached into the back of the truck for the last item we needed. A grocery sack full of Silly String.

Mel's eyes widened, and she chuckled. "Silly String?"

I grinned and wiggled my eyebrows. "I thought it would be fun to see Neil's face when he saw his precious car covered in Silly String. Then, when he washes it off—*surprise*—his paint is ruined."

Mel laughed, and I was glad to see she was no longer having reservations.

"Let's go," I said.

We were almost to the Stantons' driveway, so I put a finger to my lips. The front door was open with just a thin glass screen door separating the outside to the inside.

Neil's car was parked in the middle row of the driveway with his parents' motorhome on the far side, blocking Melanie and me from the neighbor's house. But, if someone walked out of the Stanton home, it would be hard for the two of us to hide.

I gently set the cans of Silly String on the ground, so they didn't make clanking noises against the concrete, and I went for the cap of the bottle of brake fluid.

"Why are these so hard to open?" Melanie hissed.

"I think it's because we're nervous," I answered. My hands were shaking, and my heart was racing.

I was afraid that I was going to spill the fluid all over if I continued to try to open it while standing up, so I crouched down to use the ground to keep the bottle from tipping.

Mel squatted down next to me when she saw what I was doing. My plan worked, and I was just about to stand up when I heard the screen door to the house open.

"I forgot the buns in the car. I'm grabbing them now," a voice said from the house.

It was Caleb. Apparently, ten minutes hadn't been long enough to wait.

Melanie and I froze, the look of horror on her face probably matching my own.

I put my finger to my lips. Caleb's truck was in the row closest to the house and one car back while we were between the motor home and Neil's car. If we didn't make any noise and Caleb didn't bother to look too hard, we should be safe.

I could hear Caleb open and close his truck door, and his footsteps receded back toward the house. The screen door opened and closed again, and I breathed a sigh of relief.

"That was close," Mel said.

"No kidding. I thought my heart was racing before."

"Same here."

I slowly stood, looking around to make sure no one was outside, and poured the brake fluid on the side of the car. "Make sure it doesn't cover the whole car; otherwise, it won't leave streaks in the paint."

"I remember."

It didn't take us long to empty our two little bottles of brake fluid before we took out the Silly String.

Covering Neil's car with the stuff was more fun than I'd thought it would be. Toward the end, I even drew him a special picture on the hood.

"Why did you draw a rocket?" Mel whispered.

I put the can down. "It's not a rocket. It's a dick."

Mel turned her head. "I don't see it." She looked at me. "Why did you try to draw a dick?"

"I didn't *try*." I thought it was a good rendition of the male appendage. "And I did it because Neil is a dick."

She grinned. "Good one."

"Thanks."

"We'd probably better go."

"You're right."

We made sure we didn't leave anything behind and went back to my dad's truck. We put our paraphernalia in the back, hopped in the cab, and took off.

We went to my parents' house where my car was. We changed out of our landscaper clothes, and Mel fixed her hair and makeup while I put all the evidence of our misdeeds in my parents' trash.

I said a quick hello and good-bye to my dad, who was working in the garage and who hadn't even questioned why I needed his truck. God bless the preoccupied, self-absorbed man.

Twenty minutes later, I was dropping her back off at the Stantons'.

"I'll see you around eight thirty?" I asked.

"Sounds good."

"Call me if you want me to come sooner."

"Will do." She looked at me. "We did good, right?"

"Hell yeah. The cheating scumbag won't know what hit him."

"Am I a bad person that I don't feel very guilty?"

I shook my head. "Not in the least. He really deserves a kick in the nuts. He could've had it worse."

Melanie laughed. "Thanks, Sloan."

I smiled. "Anytime. Now, go. I'll see you soon."

"I can't wait to see his reaction."

My smile turned into a grin. "Me either."

THREE
CALEB

THERE WAS A KNOCK AT MY PARENTS' front door. I was the only one in the kitchen—everyone else was in the back—so I answered it.

"Hey, Melanie."

"Hi, Caleb."

My brother's girlfriend was a tiny blonde who was one of the nicest people I knew. She was also way too good for Neil. I had no idea what she saw in him. My brother was always more interested in himself than Melanie. She deserved better.

"Everyone's out back," I told her. "My dad is grilling steaks. I hope you like them."

She smiled. "Love them."

I thought she meant it. The thing about Melanie was, she would never say that she didn't. Like I said, she was nice. She would never complain.

Yet, today, she seemed a little on edge. I hoped my brother hadn't done something stupid.

"You okay?" I asked.

"Oh, um … yeah, I'm fine."

"Okay," I said. "I'll see you out there."

Melanie went out to the backyard, and I went back to the kitchen. I snuck a bite of my mom's homemade macaroni salad—because it was my favorite—and grabbed two beers.

Once outside, I held up a beer for Melanie to see. "Do you want one?"

"Yes, please."

I handed it to her.

"Thank you."

Neil lifted his dark head from his phone and frowned at his girlfriend. "You don't drink beer."

"Yes, I do. Just not all the time." Melanie looked him in the eye and took a long sip.

I grinned behind my own bottle. I was beginning to think I might be right about the two of them having problems.

I sat down at the patio table between my mom and brother.

"So, how have you been, Melanie?" my mom asked.

"Good."

"Anything new in your life?"

Melanie took another drink of her beer. "Nothing right now."

I frowned. The way she'd said that made her sound nervous, which seemed odd.

I looked at my brother. He didn't seem to notice anything. He was too busy staring at his phone.

"And work is going well?"

My mother, bless her, was simply being polite to her

guest, but I could tell that Melanie didn't like the focus on her.

"I'm thinking about buying a house," I butted in.

My mom turned in her chair to see me better. "Caleb, that's wonderful."

Neil actually looked up from his phone at my announcement. "Are you sure you can afford it?" he asked.

I gritted my teeth. "Yes. Just because I didn't graduate college doesn't mean I don't have a good job."

Neil had graduated with an accounting degree and was a CPA. Now, he was a director of finance or something at some investment company. Truthfully, I tried to ignore him when he talked about work.

He never held back in letting everyone know that I was the screwup, the black sheep, while he was the star child. What made it even worse was that he was younger than me. Only by a year, but it still pissed me off.

"I personally think it's good for you to start looking for something permanent," my dad said from the grill. This was my dad's form of support. He wasn't giving me an *I knew you could do it* cheer, but he also wasn't telling me I couldn't the way Neil was.

"I need a real estate agent first," I said.

Melanie's eyes lit up. "Sloan is a realtor. I can give her your info if you'd like."

Neil frowned. "Don't go with her. I'll give you the name of the guy who sold me my house."

My brother was unbelievable. Not only had he totally dismissed his girlfriend's suggestion, but Sloan was also her friend.

"Sloan is a nice girl," my mother said.

I smiled at Melanie. "I would appreciate that. Please tell her I'm interested," I said even though I really didn't want to work with her friend.

Sloan was kind of standoffish, and even though I hadn't done anything to her, I could tell she didn't like me. I didn't want to work with someone difficult, but talking to her wouldn't hurt anyone. I didn't have to go with her in the end.

Melanie grinned. "You won't regret it. Her clients love her."

Maybe I had exaggerated Sloan's coldness in my head. Either way, saying yes was worth it to see the smile on Melanie's face and the scowl on Neil's.

"She's actually picking me up later tonight. You can talk to her then."

"Great," I said.

"Steaks are done," my dad said.

Dinner was delicious, and Neil actually put his phone down and talked to his family, which was a surprise.

Around eight thirty, the doorbell rang.

"I'll get it," Melanie said. "That'll be Sloan."

From the kitchen, I heard the screen door open and the two ladies talking.

"Um … Neil?" Melanie said, her voice full of worry.

My brother was still in the backyard.

"Neil," I yelled. "Melanie wants you."

"What does she want?" he yelled back.

I sighed. "He wants to know what you want, Melanie."

"Tell him something happened to his car."

I didn't even have to repeat the message. There was a

loud clank outside, and my brother came rushing through the back door.

"What's wrong?" he demanded.

"You should look outside," Sloan said. "I noticed it as I was coming up the drive."

Now, my interest was piqued, as were my parents'. We all rushed outside, and when I saw Neil's car covered in Silly String, I burst out laughing.

Neil swung around. "You did this," he accused.

"The hell I did. I was inside the house or in the backyard with you the whole night."

My brother pursed his lips. He knew I was right.

"But it doesn't mean I don't wish I had done it," I said.

"Asshole," he muttered and turned back toward his car.

Whoever had done it deserved a medal. Neil's classic car was covered in bright neon colors. There was so much Silly String; there was no way he would be able to see out of the windshield.

"Who would do such a thing?" my mother asked.

I looked at my mom. She didn't look as horrified as she'd tried to sound. I actually thought she might be trying not to laugh. My dad looked like he was biting the inside of his cheeks, too.

I stepped closer to the car and noticed something on the hood. It wasn't random Silly String. It was a drawing. "Why the hell would they draw a rocket on your car?" I asked.

"Personally, I think it looks like a dick," Sloan said, pushing her red hair off her shoulder. Her eyes widened when she noticed my parents standing there. "Sorry. I mean, wiener. Uh, no, I mean …" Her cheeks were now pink.

"We know what you meant. It's a penis," I interrupted. I

studied the thing. "It's not a very good one though."

"Who cares if there's a dick on my car?" my brother said. "What the hell am I supposed to do now?"

"I don't know." I shrugged. "Clean it."

"Do you mind if I use your bathroom?" Sloan asked my parents.

"I'll show you where it is," Melanie said.

The two went inside, and I looked at the car again and had an idea. I patted the back of my jeans. Damn. My phone was inside.

"Don't do anything yet," I told my brother. "I'll be right back."

"Why?" he asked.

No way was I telling him I needed a picture. "Just hold on."

I went into the house to search for my phone. It was by the back door, and as I picked it up, I heard Melanie and her friend.

"The look on his face was priceless," Sloan said.

"I can't believe it actually worked," Melanie said. "I was so nervous at dinner."

"Did Neil notice?"

"Nah, he was too busy staring at his phone."

"Thank God. He'd crucify us if he ever found out we were the ones who had done that to his car."

Holy shit. I couldn't believe these two were behind the prank. It seemed Melanie really was sick of her boyfriend's shit.

"I'd better get back out there," Melanie said.

"Okay. I'll be out in a second. I really do need to use the bathroom."

I waited for Melanie to go back outside before going there myself. I didn't want her to know I'd been eavesdropping. I didn't want her to worry that I would ever tell my brother it was her because he probably deserved it.

I started for the front door when my phone buzzed. It was a text message.

> Ted: Dinner is at six tomorrow night. Mary is going to make her famous lasagna. Don't forget to tell your girlfriend. I would hate for her to make other plans.

I swallowed. It was supposed to sound friendly, but I knew Ted was testing me. I'd almost forgotten about the whole find-a-girlfriend thing.

I heard the toilet flush and the sink running. And I remembered what Melanie had said about Sloan being my realtor. Maybe she could be more than that.

The door opened, and the light turned off.

Sloan walked out into the hall and stopped when she saw me. "How long have you been standing there?"

"Long enough," I told her.

She lifted her chin, and her green eyes narrowed. "How much did you hear?"

"Let's just say, I know what happened to Neil's car," I said.

She stalked toward me. "Are you going to tell?"

"That depends."

"*On what?*" she asked.

I smiled. "What if I said that I'm in need of something as much as you are? I think we can cut a deal."

Desperate times called for desperate measures after all.

FOUR
SLOAN

I CROSSED my arms over my chest. "I'm not fucking you."

Caleb took a step back as his eyebrows flew up and his eyes widened in shock. "Uh, no. Nothing sexual." He shook his head as if the idea was crazy.

I dropped my arms. "Okay." But did he have to look so revolted? I was a cute girl. Plenty of guys wanted to fuck me. "What do you want then?"

"A girlfriend."

I looked Caleb up and down. This guy didn't need help with getting a girlfriend. He was about six-two with tawny-colored hair and these big hazel eyes. I loved big eyes on men, but I would never share that with Caleb. He also had a very nice body. Muscular but not too much. Slim and trim was what I called his type. Basically, he was hot. The problem was, he probably knew it, which was why I'd stayed away from him. I'd had one too many things go wrong when it came to sexy guys.

I snorted. "I didn't think you had trouble with finding women."

"I don't," he said with a bite. "But it's more complicated than that."

Oh. The plot thickens.

"Do tell."

"No. Not until you agree."

I snorted. "You're crazy."

The sound of Neil screaming cut through the air.

Caleb and I ran to the screen door and looked outside. Neil stood with a broom in his hand and a pile of Silly String at his feet.

"*My car is ruined!*" Neil yelled. "*My paint.*"

From the corner of my eye, I saw Caleb look down at me.

"I bet you didn't know Silly String could ruin a paint job."

I'd read that in my research, but in every prank I'd seen on the internet, nothing had happened to the cars. I'd thought the Silly String had to sit on the paint a long time. A couple of hours wasn't going to do it. That was why we'd used brake fluid.

I continued looking out the door, neither confirming nor denying anything.

Caleb narrowed his eyes. "I take that back. I bet you did know that Silly String could ruin a car." He looked outside again. "But … I got here around five thirty. It hasn't been there long enough to do any real damage, which means …"

Oh jeez. The guy was good-looking and smart.

"You two did something on purpose to ruin the paint."

"You can stop thinking now," I told him.

Caleb burst out laughing.

"What do you want?"

"I already told you. I need you to play my girlfriend for a little while."

"And if I don't?"

"I'm no lawyer or police officer, but I'm pretty sure that's vandalism right there."

"So?" I looked up at Caleb. "I'd rather get arrested than pretend to date you."

He put a hand on his chest. "Ouch," he said mockingly.

I looked back outside. Neil was furious, just the way we'd wanted him to be.

"So, that's it?" Caleb said. "You'd rather go to jail than go on a few dates with me."

"Yep. And I'm sure I'd only have to pay a fine. I highly doubt I'd go to jail."

I saw Caleb shrug.

"Okay. Have it your way. But, remember, you're taking your friend down with you."

My eyes darted to Mel. She was chewing on her lip, and I knew her well enough to know she felt guilty. And the thought of the police showing up and questioning her, possibly putting her in handcuffs, made my stomach twist. I couldn't do that to her.

"How many dates?" I asked. "And when?"

"Ten. And the first date is tomorrow at my boss's house."

I looked at him. "Ten? You're out of your mind. I'll give you two."

Caleb shook his head. "No way. Ted will want to see you with me more than twice, or he'll know something's up. Eight."

"Three."

"Seven."

"Four."

"Five. Or I open this door right now and tell Neil it was you."

I took a deep breath and exhaled. "Fine. Five dates, and then we never have to see each other again."

He held out his hand. "Five dates only."

I shook it. "Five dates only."

―――――

The rest of the evening didn't go any better.

Neil called the cops, who came and took statements and pictures. I could tell they didn't care that much, but I was sure, if Caleb pointed fingers at Melanie and me, the officers would take us in for questioning.

I finally had to pull Mel away because the look of guilt on her face was bound to make others notice.

One good thing was that Caleb had kept his mouth shut, but I had to admit, I had been nervous the whole time.

When I finally heard the police drive away, I breathed a huge sigh of relief.

"I think it's time we get out of here," I told Melanie.

She nodded. "Okay."

We stood from the kitchen table as everyone else came in the house.

"We're going to take off," I told them. "Mel's ready to go home."

Melanie walked over to Neil. "I'm sorry about your car."

"It's a good thing you're going home with Sloan. I'm not good company right now."

Melanie stood on her tiptoes and kissed Neil's cheek.

He made no effort to meet her halfway, and he put his hands on her arms as if he didn't want her close to him. "You'd better go."

"I'll walk you two out," Caleb said.

"No need," I said.

"But we need to exchange phone numbers before you go."

I tried not to panic as my eyes widened. He was going to give us away.

"Oh, you must have told Sloan you wanted to buy a house," Melanie said with a small smile and started for the door.

Caleb put a hand behind my back and nudged me forward. "I did. She said she'd be happy to help me look."

"That's not part of the deal," I hissed.

Caleb put his mouth near my ear. "Oh, do you want to tell her why we need to exchange phone numbers?"

His breath tickled my neck, and I had to command my body not to shiver. It had been a long time since I had a man this close to me, but I refused to react.

"You're the one who brought up phone numbers in the first place," I quietly argued.

He was the one who had created the problem that I was now paying for.

"I'm an opportunist," he said. "Plus, I had to get your number somehow."

"What are you two whispering about?" Melanie asked.

"Sloan was just telling me she had a couple of ideas for me. We're going to meet tomorrow to go over some things."

Mel smiled. "I'm so glad. You've said sales have been down lately."

I ran my finger across my neck, but she had already pushed the door open to go outside. Meanwhile, Caleb was laughing behind me.

I turned. "I'm not meeting you tomorrow."

"How else are we supposed to get our facts straight before dinner?"

"Fine. What time? And where? I do have to show a few houses tomorrow."

He made a *come here* motion. "Give me your phone. I'll text you the details."

I unlocked my phone and reluctantly handed it over. A minute later, he handed it back.

"Can I go now?" I asked.

He walked over to the door and opened it. "I'll see you tomorrow."

"Yeah, yeah," I said, stomping out of the house.

A second later, my phone buzzed in my hand. I had a message from...

> Lover: How about a Starbucks or Caribou around ten a.m.? Will that work for you?

I turned around, scowled, and held up my phone as I shook it back and forth. "I'm changing it to *Loser* as soon as I get home."

I could hear Caleb laugh through the glass.

I hated that I couldn't faze him.

FIVE

CALEB

THE NEXT MORNING, I looked at my watch for the umpteenth time. It was ten minutes after ten with no sign of Sloan.

I hoped she hadn't called my bluff.

Because, even if she didn't show up today, I wasn't going to tell my brother or turn her and Melanie over to the police. My brother was an asshole and had probably done something shitty. He'd never had a reputation as a good boyfriend.

I had even enjoyed watching him get pissed off myself.

But I needed Sloan to think that I would turn her in, so she would go through with our deal.

I *needed* Ted to take me seriously. I wanted nothing more than to buy his shop from him and take care of it till the day I died. But I needed him to see that, too.

I sighed and pulled out my phone to send Sloan a text when she breezed through the door.

She held up a finger. "I'll be right back," she said and

went to the counter to put in her order as I watched her from afar.

She was medium height and thin. Usually, I preferred a little meat and booty on the women I dated, but Sloan was pretty with her red hair and dark green eyes. I didn't think anyone would question me liking her.

Several minutes later, she walked up to the table, a large coffee or latte in her hand.

I kicked her chair out from under the table for her. "Have a seat," I said with a smile.

"You're such a gentleman," she said as she sat.

I shrugged a shoulder. "We've been dating a couple of months. I'm done playing the gentleman."

"You're a prick," she said, and I laughed.

Truth be told, I liked teasing her. If she really were my girlfriend, I would show her that I could indeed be a gentleman. But, somewhere along the line, Sloan had decided I wasn't worth her time, and it seemed only fitting that I lived up to her expectations.

Besides, if I was going to have a fake girlfriend, I might as well make it fun.

I leaned forward on the table. "I figured we could work out some technical stuff. I'm sure Ted and his wife will have plenty of questions for us." I quickly explained my work dilemma and why I needed a girlfriend.

"Okay, where should we start?"

"I was thinking we start with how we met."

"Okay. The best thing is to stick with the truth. My friend is dating your brother. We met about a year and a half ago, I suppose."

"'I suppose.' That's good. Keep it general. It sounds more realistic." I nodded.

"When did we start dating?" she asked.

"Good question. I told Ted that I was serious about you, yet I'd obviously never brought you up before."

"Why don't we say about two and a half months? Long enough to develop feelings, but not so long that everyone should have met me by now."

I smiled. "Perfect. Two and a half months it is."

"Where did you take me on our first date?" She held up a finger. "Our first *real* date. Not the couple of times we hung out with Melanie and Neil, which is how we realized we liked each other, by the way."

"Wow. Nice background. I like it."

This girl was good.

"So, where did you take me on our first date?"

"To dinner. It's a classic; plus, we both love food." I lifted a brow. "At least, I think we do."

"I do love food. Good guess. But where did you take me?"

"What's your favorite restaurant? Oh, and we're having lasagna tonight. I hope you like it."

"That's cheating. The guy should come up with the restaurant for the first date. No fishing for ideas. And, yes, lasagna sounds delicious."

"Not if we were friends, hanging out with Melanie and Neil. I probably would have learned your favorite restaurant from just talking to you," I said.

"Good point. I love Crave."

"Crave it is."

"What did we do after?"

"Made out in my car?" I joked.

Sloan rolled her eyes. "What are we, in high school?"

I laughed. "How about we just walked around downtown Minneapolis, going into stores and just hanging out?"

"I suppose that could work," she agreed.

"What's your favorite food?"

"Pizza."

"Perfect. Mine, too. What's your favorite color?"

"Black."

"Like your heart. Easy to remember. Mine is blue." I took a drink of my coffee.

Sloan gave me the finger.

"Is that coffee in there?" I pointed to her cup.

"Yes. Coffee is life."

"Another thing we have in common," I said. "Siblings? You obviously know mine."

"I have a younger brother, Travis. He's a personal trainer. He's married to Sydney."

"Okay. Easy enough to remember. When's your birthday?"

"February 18. I'm thirty."

"Got it." It was July. We hadn't been dating when she had her birthday, so that was one less important event to remember. "Mine is October 13. I'm thirty-one."

"What about college? That's something people know about each other. I have a two-year degree in business from Hennepin Technical College. Then, I studied and took the test to be a realtor, and I've been doing that since I was twenty-one. My mom is a realtor, so for the first few years, I helped her and learned the ropes before I branched out on my own. You?"

"I went to Minnesota State for two years. I majored in marketing. But I quit after my second year and decided to go to Europe for a year. When I came back, I started working full-time at the sporting goods store, made my way up to manager, and decided it wasn't worth it to return to school."

Sloan tilted her head. "Why did you quit in the first place? Why did you decide to travel halfway around the world?"

I looked away from her and out a window. "My grandfather died. I'd always been close to him. He was the one who had convinced me to go to college, and when he died, I just didn't see the point anymore." Every time I had thought of going back after that summer, I'd felt sick. It'd remind me of my grandpa. I had needed to get away to someplace that wouldn't remind me of him. Europe seemed almost far enough away. I cleared my throat. "I don't really like talking about it."

"I understand. I was close to both my grandparents before they passed away, too."

I looked at her and smiled weakly. "Can you think of anything else? Any other basics we need to cover?"

She leaned forward. "Yes. You need to tell me what kind of house you want to buy."

I curled my lip. "Do we really have to do that? A lot of that was talk."

She smiled. "Either you buy a house through me or I'll let your secret out to your boss tonight, cops be damned."

I raised my brow. "Okay then." I started giving her a list

of what I wanted if I was to buy a house, and she got out a piece of paper and wrote it all down. "It's actually a good thing my new girlfriend sells real estate. It'll make it more believable as one reason that I'm buying a house now."

"I think we'll do fine tonight. Is there anything else you need?" She looked at her watch. "I have to meet a client in a half an hour."

"Are you always busy on the weekend with work?"

"If I don't make plans, I do show a lot of houses. People don't work on weekends, so it's a good time."

"That's good to know. I also work weekends, about every third."

She tapped her head. "I've got all the info saved." Sloan stood and slung her purse over her shoulder. "Anything else?"

"One more thing," I said in a serious tone. "This is important."

"What is it?"

I motioned toward me. "Come closer."

She put an arm on the table and leaned over.

"Just in case anyone asks …" I looked around the room to make sure that no one was listening.

"What? Just tell me."

I met Sloan's eyes and grinned. "In case anyone asks, I think you should know, I have a big dick."

"Ugh," she groaned as she pushed herself off the table. "You're a pervert," she said as she turned and headed for the door.

"I just thought you should get your facts straight," I called out to her. "I don't want you to sell me short."

Sloan shook her head and pushed the door open.

"Get it? Sell me short."

Sloan walked away as I took a long drink of my coffee. Goading her was so much fun.

SIX

SLOAN

CALEB RANG THE DOORBELL, and we waited for his boss to answer.

"Now, remember, you're my girlfriend. If I put my arm around you or kiss your cheek, it's because I'm playing the part. I am not hitting on you."

"I know."

"And please try not to flinch when I get close to you."

I frowned. "I won't."

Caleb snorted. "We'll see."

Footsteps sounded from the other side of the door.

"Showtime," he said and put his arm around me.

I stiffened.

"Loosen up," Caleb said from the side of his mouth. "While I like being right, I'd love for you to prove me wrong tonight."

Damn.

He was right. I needed to get over my resistance to men.

I took a deep breath, relaxed into him, and put my arm around his waist.

Wow. No body fat on this guy.

The door swung open, and a man with salt-and-pepper hair stood on the other side. "Caleb and …"

"This is Sloan," Caleb said.

"Come in, come in."

Caleb dropped his arm from around me and put it at the small of my back as we walked inside. The house was stunning. Big and spacious. My realtor brain was automatically calculating how much the place would cost to buy. It wouldn't be cheap.

I held out my hand. "It's lovely to meet you. I've heard nice things about you. And you have a beautiful home."

"Thank you. It's nice to meet you, too," Ted said. "And I wish I could say the same about hearing nice things about you."

I laughed and put my hand on Caleb's arm. "I heard he's been keeping me a secret around the water cooler."

Caleb scowled. "I wasn't ready to tell everyone yet."

I couldn't tell if he was acting or not.

I put my arm around him again and smiled up at him. "Well, I'm glad you finally did." I looked at Ted. "And thank you for inviting me tonight."

"It's my pleasure. Why don't you come into the sitting room?" Ted said and showed us the way. Once we reached the room, he asked, "What can I get you to drink? Beer? Wine? Pop? Water?"

"I'll take a beer," Caleb said, "and Sloan will have white wine."

Ted smiled. "I'll be right back."

Caleb poked his head out of the room and spun around. "Way to prove me wrong. You did good back there."

"I know." I narrowed my eyes and put my hands on my hips. "But why did you just assume I wanted wine? Is that because it's what all women drink?" My tone had a bite to it.

Caleb rolled his eyes. "Relax. I wasn't assuming anything. I've seen you drink wine more than once at Melanie's house."

I dropped my arms. "Oh."

"You're determined to hate me, aren't you?"

"I am not."

"Could have fooled me."

It wasn't that I wanted to hate him so much as I didn't want to like him. Men were trouble, and while I could try to keep myself rational when it came to the opposite sex, my heart and my vagina often overruled my head. It was easier to keep my distance, which was even easier if I didn't like someone.

But what I really didn't like was that he'd remembered I drank wine. He wasn't supposed to remember anything about me.

"Here come the drinks," Ted said as he entered the room with a woman behind him.

She had two glasses of wine, and she handed one to me. "I'm Mary, Ted's wife."

I smiled. "Nice to meet you. Thank you for the invite. And thank you for cooking."

"You are more than welcome, dear." She walked over to Caleb, and they kissed each other on the cheek. "I like her already," she told him.

Caleb smiled. "Your approval's all I need, Mar."

Mary laughed and held out her hand. "Sit, you two. This is supposed to be a relaxing night."

There were two love seats with a coffee table in the middle, and Caleb sat on one. I was about to sit on the one opposite him when he lifted an eyebrow.

I quickly hightailed it over to him and parked my butt while Mary and Ted sat across from us.

"How long have you known each other?" Mary asked.

I pretended to think about it because, to me, it seemed more realistic. If I just blurted out the answer, it might sound like we'd rehearsed. "We met when my friend started dating Caleb's brother." I looked at him. "So, it's been about a year and a half. Right, honey?"

Caleb had been taking a drink of his beer and started coughing when I called him honey. He wiped the side of his mouth with his thumb. "That sounds about right."

Mary looked surprised. "And you've been dating this whole time?"

"Oh my, no," I said. "We've only been seeing each other for about two or three months."

"I would never be able to keep someone like Sloan a secret for over a year."

The three of us laughed, but Ted said, "That's a good thing because it wasn't that long ago that he brought another girl by the shop. I think her name was Tiffany."

Caleb looked uncomfortable, and while I couldn't be sure, I was pretty confident Ted was testing Caleb and me.

I shooed my hand in front of me. "She's got nothing on me, Ted."

Caleb relaxed, and Ted smiled.

A buzzer sounded from another room, and Mary stood.

"Dinner's ready. Ted, will you show them to the dining room?"

Dinner was delicious, and despite the continuous quizzing, I was actually enjoying myself. I swirled my glass of wine in my hand. Of course, that could be all the alcohol talking.

We were finishing up, and I wiped my mouth and set my napkin on my plate. "That was delicious, Mary. I don't think I've ever had homemade lasagna. I'm never going to want to eat it at a restaurant again."

Mary grinned. "Thank you. You're more than welcome to come and eat anytime."

I leaned over and put my head on Caleb's shoulder. "You must bring me here every time this is on the menu."

He smiled down at me, and I couldn't help but notice how beautiful he looked. My eyes moved down to his mouth, and I wondered what his lips tasted like.

"You don't have to have Caleb bring you. You can come here on your own," Mary said.

I lifted my head and gasped. "Really? That's so nice of you."

Caleb leaned close to my ear. "I think you'd better lay off the wine."

His breath was hot on my neck, and I shivered. It had been a long time since I was kissed there.

I grabbed for my glass. *Oh jeez.* I should not be thinking about kissing and necks. I smiled at him. "I'm fine, thank you." I patted him on the knee. "Besides, you're driving."

Ted and Mary laughed, and I beamed at their approval. I liked these two.

"How does dessert sound?" Mary asked.

"Delicious," I said.

"You didn't make anything with eggs, right?" Caleb asked, his tone full of concern. "I texted Ted to tell you that Sloan is allergic to eggs."

Mary smiled at the two of us, but I barely noticed.

Caleb had remembered I was allergic to eggs. That was so sweet.

It probably didn't sound sweet to everyone, but when someone remembered you had a life-threatening allergy and went out of their way to make sure you could eat with the rest of the group, it was very considerate.

Some people treated me like not eating certain things was a choice. When I was a kid, I'd hated going to birthday parties and being the only one who couldn't eat the cake. It had always made me feel like an outsider.

"Yes, Caleb," Mary said, "I remembered. We're having apple pie and ice cream. No eggs in either. I even made sure the lasagna noodles didn't have eggs in them." She stood. "Ted, will you come and help me?"

"I can help you," I quickly volunteered.

"No, no. You are a guest. You sit and relax," Mary told me.

I could tell she meant business. "Okay," I said with a smile. But I was definitely bringing my dirty dishes to the kitchen when we were done eating.

Ted and Mary left the dining room, and I looked at Caleb.

"What?" he asked. "Do I have food on my face or something?" He picked up his napkin and ran it across his mouth.

I smiled. "No. Thank you for telling them about my allergy."

He grinned. "Now, I know you really are drunk."

"Why is that?"

"Because you just thanked me."

"Ha-ha."

He leaned closer. "And you're welcome. I want a fake girlfriend, not a dead date." He ran his thumb over my chin. "But, right now, I need to use the bathroom. I'll be right back."

Ted came back to the dining room first. "Mary's bringing it all out at the same time."

"That's fine. I can wait," I assured him.

"I hope you didn't have to cancel plans last minute to come tonight."

"I was supposed to show a few houses, but I just moved some things around."

"Show houses?"

"Yes, I'm a realtor."

Ted started nodding. "I see. And Caleb is buying a house from you?"

"He'd better, or I've been wasting my time these past couple of weeks." I laughed at my joke. And I mentally patted myself on the back for my quick reply, as if I'd been showing him houses for a while now.

But Ted barely smiled. "Did Caleb convince you to play the role of his girlfriend tonight?"

I froze. "Excuse me?" So much for singing my own praises. I had no idea how to respond.

"Did Caleb influence you to play the role of his girl-friend tonight? Maybe in exchange for spending more money?"

"Theodore Goldman, I'm ashamed of you. Caleb is like the son we never had," Mary said from behind Ted as she came in the room with the dessert.

Ted helped her set it on the table. "Honey, you know I love Caleb, and that's why I'm asking these questions. I know how much he wants the store, but I want to make sure he really wants it. He might be the son I never had, but that store is my baby."

I was still sitting in my seat with my mouth hanging open, in shock that Ted would ask that question of me. Both those questions.

And, while I could confess everything right then, some-thing inside me went the extreme opposite, and I defended Caleb. Later, I would blame it on his memory of my aller-gies and all the wine. I was feeling sentimental.

"No, Caleb didn't offer to buy a bigger house in exchange for me playing his girlfriend. We really are dating. In fact, we're looking at a house to buy together because we're actually talking about marriage."

The minute it left my mouth, I realized I'd said the wrong thing.

Mary gasped, and her hands flew to her mouth. She grinned, and a tear slid down her face. "I'm so happy," she said when she finally pulled her hands away.

"What's going on?" Caleb said when he entered the room.

Mary ran over to him and flung her arms around him. "You've made my week, Caleb."

46

Caleb looked at me, but his whole body was jarred when Ted slapped him on the back.

"Congratulations, son."

Caleb's eyes brightened. "Does this mean you're going to let me buy the store?"

Ted laughed and wagged his finger. "I'm still thinking about that. No, I'm talking about your other news. Sloan just told us."

Caleb's eyes flew to mine. "What did she tell you?"

"That you're engaged," Ted said.

"We're so happy for you," Mary said.

I picked up my glass of wine and tried to bury my face in it.

SEVEN
CALEB

I WAITED for about ten seconds after we drove away from Ted and Mary's before I shouted, "Engaged! *What in the hell were you thinking?*"

Sloan shrugged like it was no big deal. "I could see that Ted didn't believe you. I had to say something. And what I actually said was that we were *talking* about getting married. Ted and Mary were the ones who spun it into an engagement. As you can see, it's not totally my fault."

"Damn it, Sloan. It doesn't matter that you didn't come out and say the word *engaged*. You just made this situation way more complicated. I was going to tell Ted we broke up a few months from now. But, now, when I tell him we broke off our engagement, he's never going to believe that we were actually together." I narrowed my eyes. "Is that why you made up the lie? So that I'd get caught?"

She patted my hand. "Relax, Caleb. We'll find some excuse as to why we broke it off." She leaned forward. "Hey, I know. We could tell him that you cheated on me."

I gave her a dirty look. "I don't cheat. *Ever*. And I

certainly wouldn't cheat on the woman I loved and asked to spend the rest of my life with me."

She blew out a breath and sat back in her seat. "Maybe you got cold feet, and cheating was a way to end it."

"No way. Cheating is a hard no."

I'd been cheated on in high school, and I still remembered the awful feeling of finding out. I'd sworn, I would never do that to anyone, and I hadn't. And I wasn't about to start now. Real or fake relationship.

I smirked. "I know. Why don't we say that *you* cheated on *me*?"

Sloan scoffed. "I would never."

"Oh, so it's okay for me to be a cheater but not you?"

She stuck her nose in the air. "Men are notorious cheaters. It just makes sense it would be you."

"You sound like you're speaking from experience rather than cold, hard facts."

"Forget it." She crossed her arms across her chest. "No cheating by either of us." She dropped her arms. "Speaking of, does that mean no dating while this whole fake relationship is going on? Because, if someone saw you with another girl, it could ruin your plans."

"Same for you. Are you worried you can't keep it in your pants?"

She gasped. "How rude. I have no problem with keeping it in my pants. If you knew how long I'd already been going without sex, you'd be amazed."

"More like horrified," I said and made a mental note to find out how long it had been for her. I was curious, but at the moment, I was still more angry than interested in her celibacy. "How did we get engaged anyway?"

"I don't know. I'm guessing you got down on one knee."

"No, not how did we get fake engaged. How did it come about tonight that you told them we were getting married?"

"Oh. I told Ted I was in real estate, and he figured out I was your realtor. Then, he asked if you had offered to buy a bigger house from me in exchange for me playing your girlfriend. I was insulted that he thought you would bribe me and that I would go along with it—"

"Blackmail's okay, but bribery is a no-go," I interrupted with sarcasm.

"*You* blackmailed me. It's not the same as me accepting a bribe."

"Whatever."

"Anyway, as I was saying, I was insulted, so I told him we were talking about marriage and looking for a house together."

I put my finger up. "Repeat that last part."

"He thought you were bribing me. It was insulting."

"After that."

"I told him we were thinking about marriage," she said, confusion in her tone.

I took a deep breath. "You told him we were talking about marriage and what else?"

I looked over at Sloan, and I could see she'd finally figured out what I was asking. She suddenly looked guilty.

"I told him we were buying a house together."

The light in front of me turned red, and I slammed on my brakes. "*What the actual fuck?*" I slowly looked over at Sloan. "Now, we're buying a house together, too?"

She shrugged. "You need to relax."

I didn't think this girl could have dug a deeper hole if

50

she'd tried. The light turned green, and I accelerated. There was one thing she could have mentioned, I realized.

"Why didn't you just tell him you were pregnant, too, while you were at it?"

Her jaw dropped. "I was drinking."

"I could have told Ted and Mary that you were an alcoholic and trying to quit." An idea came to me. "Maybe that's why I leave you. You can't stay away from the sauce, and I leave your ass."

"I am not an alcoholic, and I would never drink while pregnant." She pointed a finger at me. "And so help me, if you tell them that I am, I will reveal your secret. Jail or no jail."

Wow. She really meant that.

I pushed her hand down. "Relax. Plenty of people are alcoholics. As long as they're getting help and not hurting anybody, it's nothing to be ashamed of. It is a disease after all."

"I still refuse for that to be the reason we break it off," she said, her voice firm.

I could tell I'd really struck a nerve. "Okay, no alcoholism. For either of us."

She narrowed her eyes at me. "Promise?"

"Yes, I promise." I looked her up and down. "Maybe no more drinking when we're on our dates. You get too emotional."

"You're a jerk."

"You're only proving my point," I said. "Why can't you be like most dates and want to have sex when you drink? It would be so much better than having you make up lies and threaten to reveal our secret."

She swung her head up and wrinkled her nose at me. "Ew. I don't want to have sex with you."

"Yeah, well, I don't really want to have sex with you right now either. In fact, I'm so stressed out that I'll probably never get hard again."

Sloan's eyes cut to the top of my pants.

I quickly put my hand on top of dick. "What are you doing? You can't look at my crotch."

It was a good thing I had a hand on my lap because Little Caleb liked Sloan looking, and he wanted to stand up and say hi.

Down, asshole.

Sloan laughed at my discomfort. "I guess I'm just thinking how much bullshit you fed me at the coffee shop today," she said.

I pulled in front of Sloan's house and put my truck in park. "Bullshit?"

"Yeah, about you having a big dick."

"Ah … that. I was lying," I lied.

Maybe Sloan *was* like other drunk people and did get horny when she drank. But I didn't want to find out. I was stone-cold sober, and I wouldn't take advantage of her like that.

Besides, sleeping together would complicate things, and Sloan had done enough complicating tonight already.

"I think you're lying now," she said in a husky voice with a sexy smile on her face.

My *oh shit* meter began to ring.

I leaned as far away from her as I could. "Think what you want. But my dick is little. Tiny. I shouldn't even call it a dick; it's so small."

"Are you sure about that?" she asked, a sly smile on her face.

"Never been surer in my life."

Sloan lost her sexy look and grinned. She pulled out her phone, showed me the screen, and hit stop on her voice recorder. "Now, I have something on you, too. I raise your blackmail for mine. I don't want to do this anymore. All we do is fight. You get one more date, forget the other three, and we'll come up with a good lie together about our breakup. Agree, or I'm posting this to social media." She hit play, and my voice came out, telling her how small my dick was.

I shook my head and chuckled. "You're good; I'll give you that. The thing is, I already told you that you'd put us in a real predicament tonight." I shrugged. "And, well"—I reached out, grabbed her phone, and hit delete—"I just can't let you leave me hanging like that. A deal's a deal." I hit record. "And I was lying about lying. My dick is huge." I hit stop and threw the cell in her lap.

"I hate you," she said and kicked the passenger door open harder than necessary.

"Right now, the feeling's mutual, babe."

EIGHT
SLOAN

I WAS STILL upset with Caleb when I woke up the next morning, although I tried not to be. He didn't know about my cousin and her trouble with alcoholism. But then I remembered that he was the one who'd put me in the weird predicament of playing his girlfriend, and he didn't deserve my sympathy. But I also had to admit, I had made everything worse by adding the engaged aspect and us buying a house together.

Needless to say, when it came to Caleb, I had a lot of mixed feelings and emotions going on in my head, so for the rest of the weekend, I chose to pretend they didn't exist.

By Tuesday, I was calmer, and I'd decided two things. The better I threw myself into the girlfriend thing, the sooner we could do our five dates, and the closer I'd be to ending the whole charade. The other thing was, I needed to put some of my focus on the work aspect of our relationship. I was going to find the perfect house for Caleb, and he was going to buy it from me, damn it.

The only problem was, I had no idea what area he wanted to live in or how much he wanted to spend.

I pulled my phone off my desk and sent a text to Caleb.

> Me: How much are you looking to spend on a house? Where would you like to live?

I did some other work that I needed to finish that morning, including doing a walk-through for a closing I had that week, without hearing back from Caleb. I was trying not to get irritated, but I wanted to start doing a search for him. So, next, I sent a message to Melanie.

> Me: Do you know where Caleb lives?

> Melanie: Why?

I explained how I was going to use his current address as a place to start my search.

> Melanie: Did you talk about this on Saturday when you met with him?

I sighed. I was going to have to tell Mel about me being Caleb's fake girlfriend. I wouldn't tell her about the blackmail though. I would just tell her I was helping out as a friend. But I wasn't going to tell her today.

> Me: Long story. I'll tell you about it later.

> Melanie: Ooh. Now, I'm intrigued.

> Me: Don't be. It's boring. Now, do you know where he lives?

She gave me his address, and I wrote it down in my notes I'd started for him.

> Me: Thank you.

I looked up Caleb's address and saw that he lived in an apartment, and I found the apartment's website. I didn't know if he lived in a one- or two-bedroom, but the monthly rent for both wasn't that big of a difference.

After doing some calculations, I figured out a reasonable price range for Caleb that I could start with until I actually spoke to him.

My phone buzzed.

> Melanie: You're welcome. Are you going to start showing him today?

> Me: I don't know. He won't respond to my texts.

> Melanie: He's probably at work.

Or avoiding me. I looked at the time. I had a couple of hours before I had to meet with another client. Maybe I could go to Caleb's work and force him to set up a time to see houses.

I smiled. He did want me to play his girlfriend. A nagging girlfriend sounded like a lot of fun.

Me: Thanks. I'll wait until later to talk to him then.

Melanie: Good luck.

I didn't let myself leave for Caleb's work until I found five reasonable listings. I had a feeling he was going to shoot me down, so if I could negotiate two or three out of the five, I would be happy.

The store was easy enough to find, and the parking lot wasn't full. For a moment, I wondered why he wanted to buy the place. However, it was the middle of the day during the week. It was probably busier on weeknights and weekends. Either way, the sparsely filled parking lot was a good sign for me. Caleb couldn't ignore me if there weren't any customers.

I walked into the store and was immediately surprised at how large the space was. I had pictured it smaller in my head. I knew they sold used sports equipment, but I hadn't realized they sold used exercise equipment, too. Treadmills, ellipticals, and bikes lined up almost one whole side of the store.

"Can I help you?" a young lady asked as she approached me. The tag on her shirt said her name was Leah.

"Yes. I'm looking for Caleb." I almost asked if he was working that day, but I caught myself just in time. A girlfriend or fiancée would know when her man worked.

Leah stood on her tiptoes and looked around. "I think he might be in the back. I'll go get him."

"Thank you," I told her.

After Leah walked away, I glanced around the store. I

was checking out an elliptical when I heard someone say my name. I turned around to see Ted.

I smiled. "Hello."

"What are you doing here, young lady?"

"I came to persuade Caleb to look at some houses with me after he gets off work today." I leaned toward Ted and whispered, "Maybe you can help me convince him."

Ted laughed. "Like pulling teeth, huh?"

I rolled my eyes. "Ugh. You wouldn't believe it. I just don't get it. Looking for a new house is fun."

"I can understand where Caleb is coming from. That's why Mary and I have been in the same house for twenty years."

I laughed.

"Sloan? What are you doing here?"

I looked over to see Caleb's surprised face as he approached Ted and me.

"She wants to take you house-hunting this evening," Ted said as Caleb reached us.

"I tried texting you. I was beginning to think you were ignoring me." I slid over to his side, put my arm around him, and arched up to kiss him on the mouth. It was what a normal girlfriend would do. Unfortunately, the spark I felt when our lips touched cleared all thoughts from my brain.

Caleb tilted his head to the side with his brow raised, and I realized that he'd said something to me. I'd completely missed it.

"I'm sorry. What did you say?"

He lifted his eyebrows. "I didn't have my phone on me. I would never ignore my *fiancée*," he said.

Just your fake one, I thought.

"Besides, I can't go tonight. I already have plans with Greg. Remember?"

Damn. I had to think quick. I should have known that he already had plans.

I hit my head with the heel of my hand that wasn't still around his hip. "That's right. I'm all messed up on my days. It's only Tuesday."

"You can leave early today," Ted said. "I can cover the floor for you."

Caleb's hand tightened around my waist. I had a feeling he didn't want to go with me.

I put my head on Caleb's chest. *Wow.* He smelled good.

"Uh, that is so sweet of you, Ted. But I'm actually working with a couple this afternoon."

I felt Caleb relax.

Ha. I'm not letting you off that easy.

I looked up at him. "What about tomorrow night?" I stuck out my lip.

Caleb glanced at Ted and then back at me. "Okay, tomorrow night."

I grinned. "It's a date."

Caleb smiled and waved his finger in front of my face. "Uh-uh-uh. It's house-hunting. It is *definitely* not a date."

I had known he would probably say something like that, but I'd had to try.

"What are you two doing this weekend?" Ted asked.

"I'd have to look at my calendar," I said. "Why? Did you change your mind about buying a house?" I joked.

Ted laughed. "No. Mary and I are going to our lake cabin this weekend. You two should come up."

A whole weekend with Caleb? Pass.

"Oh, I—"

"We'd love to," Caleb said, cutting me off. He squeezed my side again.

"But I have plans," I lied. Kind of. I had cleared my weekend for a couple coming from out of town, but last night, they had canceled on me. So, my new plans were to sit on my butt and watch Netflix.

"What plans?" Caleb asked.

"Uh … um … Melanie and I …"

"Oh, come on, baby. It's only summer for a little while. We should go to the lake before it gets cold. You'll love it. It'll be a date," he said.

That would be one more out of the way.

"How far is the drive?" I asked Ted.

"About an hour, hour and a half."

I looked at Caleb. "I'll go up one day. We can drive up in the morning and drive home that night. I'll move all my plans to the day we don't go."

"Deal. What day do you want to go?"

"Saturday work for you?" I asked him.

Caleb looked at Ted. "We'll be there on Saturday."

I extracted myself from Caleb's embrace. I'd gotten what I wanted. House-searching plans. I didn't even have to pull up any of the properties I'd found. And he'd gotten what he wanted. Another date. It was time for me to leave.

"I'd better go. It was nice talking to you again, Ted. I'll see you on Saturday." I turned to Caleb and poked him in the chest. "And I'll see you later. Maybe tonight?" I said for Ted's advantage. Let him think Caleb was coming over to spend the night with me. "If not tonight, I'll see you tomorrow after work."

"Yes, you will," he said and looked like he really meant it.

I dropped my arm and took a step back. "Later then." I turned.

"Sloan?" Caleb said.

I swung back. "Yeah?"

"You forgot to kiss me good-bye." He grinned.

I rolled my eyes, so only Caleb could see and moved toward him again.

I went in for the same kind of peck I'd given him when I first arrived, but Caleb cupped my chin between his thumb and forefinger and opened my mouth for him. His tongue slipped inside, and I moaned.

Oh God. He's a good kisser.

I hadn't been kissed like this in a long, long time.

A throat cleared, and my senses returned swiftly. I quickly took a step back.

"Sorry, Ted," Caleb said. He turned his gaze to me and smiled. His look told me that he was anything but remorseful.

I took another step back and ran into a rack of workout pants. "Sorry." I turned and made sure I hadn't knocked anything to the ground. "I'd better go." I walked toward the door. "See you later," I called over my shoulder without glancing back.

When I got to my car, I inspected my image in my rearview mirror. I looked the same. I couldn't let one kiss affect me.

I pulled out my phone and brought up Caleb's number.

Me: No more kissing.

Two seconds later.

Caleb: No promises. It's what couples do.

So much for him not having his phone with him. He *had* been ignoring me.

Me: Fine. Kissing only when others are around. But no tongue. And, next time, answer my texts, so I don't have to show up at your work.

Caleb: Kinky. I never took you for a voyeur, but if that's the way you want it. Kissing only in front of others. Lots of tongue. Got it.

Me: Quit twisting my words around.

Caleb: I have to go back to work. Talk to you later, baby.

I really hated it when he got the last word.

NINE
CALEB

I STOPPED at the front door of the sixth house Sloan had brought me to when I realized she was leaning up against the side of the house, staring at her phone.

"You're not coming in with me?" I asked.

"Why bother?" she said, her eyes not leaving her phone. "You haven't liked a single one. We spend more time driving place to place than you do checking it out."

I shrugged. "I know what I like and don't like. If I don't like something, why bother sticking around?"

She looked up at me and tilted her head. "But will you ever like something?"

"I'm sure I will."

"We'll see." She waved her hand. "Go. Look around. Hate, so we can move on to the next place. I'm getting hungry."

I quickly walked through the house, like the five before, and walked out the front door.

Sloan put her phone down and pushed away from the wall. "I didn't want to be right, but it appears that I was."

"I'm sorry. It's just not me."

"Well, maybe, if you gave me a little more detail about what is you, then I would know what to search for."

I nodded my head. "Okay. Let's go to dinner first." I grabbed her hand and started for her car.

She pulled her arm away. "No. No dates tonight. I can't. I am way too tired."

"It's not a date. It's just two friends having dinner. We'll go somewhere no one knows us. There'll be no pretending. We'll just relax and eat. Maybe talk about house stuff." I shrugged. "Or maybe we won't. It's up to you."

She peered at me out of the corner of her eyes. "We're friends now?"

"We could be if we stopped fighting."

"Friends don't blackmail friends."

I laughed. "That sounds like a conversation to have over food and drinks."

"I thought you said no more drinking?"

"On our dates. This isn't a date, remember?"

She stood there, and I could practically see her making a list of pros and cons.

"Okay. I'm starving, and I don't want to go home and cook."

"Great." I walked over to the passenger door. "Where do you want to go?"

"What restaurant do you hate?"

"Buffalo Wild Wings. It's too loud."

Sloan grinned. "Great. Let's go there."

"What if I say no?"

She unlocked her car. "What if I told you I know it's

actually one of your favorite restaurants?" She opened her door and got behind the wheel.

I opened my door and slid inside. "Then, I'd accuse you of stalking me, and I'd tell you where the nearest one is."

She turned the engine over and backed out of the drive-way. She stopped and stared at me. "I already know where the nearest one is. And, if I were stalking you, you'd never even suspect," she said in a serious tone.

I chuckled nervously. "I know you're joking, but you're kind of scaring me, too."

She laughed, put the car in drive, and hit the gas. "Good."

"I think I just heard you cackle."

Sloan laughed again, and I grabbed on to the nearest handle.

"Feeling better?" I asked as Sloan pushed away her almost-empty plate.

"Yes."

I smiled. "I'm glad." I pushed my own plate out of the way and rested my arms on the table. "Would you like to talk houses?"

"Sure." She reached over to the nearby chair where her purse sat and took out a notebook and pencil. "Let's start with neighborhoods and prices."

"I noticed you tried to get close to where I live now, but I don't need to live there. Ideally, I'd like to live as close to the store as possible."

Sloan looked up from her pad of paper. "Even if you don't get to buy it?"

I winced. "I'd hate to think that it wasn't an option, but yes. It's still a good job, and it pays me well."

"Unless the new owner fires you."

"Now, why'd you go and have to say something like that?"

She shrugged. "It could happen."

I tilted my head. "You're kind of a Negative Nancy."

Sloan frowned. "I am not."

"I think I'm going to start calling you Cynical Sloan."

"Those two words don't start with the same letter."

"Who cares? It has a ring to it. Cynical Sloan. I like it."

"I don't. Can we just get on with the house stuff?"

"Right. Yes. I'd like a three-bedroom, two baths at least."

Sloan wrote down what I'd said and looked up again. "Can I ask why? You're only one person."

"Two reasons. It'll sell faster if it has at least three bedrooms. And it might not always be me. If I find someone and get married, we could live there for a few years before we had a bunch of kids. And I can go about fifty thousand more than the houses we looked at today."

She raised her eyebrows. "A bunch of kids?"

I laughed. "Okay. I was thinking one or two."

"I never took you for the type of guy who wanted all that stuff."

I frowned. "Why not?"

She shrugged. "I don't know. I'm just surprised, I guess."

"Don't you want all that stuff?"

She shrugged again. "I don't know. At one time, I did, but ..."

"But what?" A disturbing thought occurred to me. I leaned in closer and lowered my voice. "Did someone hurt you?"

I could admit it; Sloan wasn't my favorite person, but the thought of someone hurting her pissed me off.

She sighed. "Just my bank account, my pride, and my ability to trust my taste in men."

"Is that why you haven't had sex in a long time?"

Her eyes narrowed. "How do you know that?"

"You told me."

"When?" she accused.

"The night of our first date."

She sat there, and I could tell she was trying to remember everything we'd talked about. "Oh, yeah. I guess I drank more than I thought."

"I suppose that's why you tried to blackmail me back. Thankfully, you were drunk enough for me to grab your phone."

Sloan chuckled. "Yeah, that wasn't my finest moment." Her smile dropped. "But I was mad at you."

"I was mad at you, too."

I could see this conversation going one of two ways. Either we started fighting again or we made a truce. And, seeing as how I'd started the whole thing, I should offer up peace.

"I'm sorry I yelled at you that night. I was panicked and worried, but it didn't give me a right to holler at you. I know you were trying to help. You could have ratted me out instead, but you didn't."

Sloan stared at me, and I had no idea what she was thinking.

"Also, I'm sorry I blackmailed you into being my girl-friend. That was wrong of me. I know we don't know each other that well, but I should have just asked you to help me out rather than forcing you."

She still didn't speak.

"Will you please say something?"

"I'm just trying to see if you really mean it."

I sat back in my chair and rolled my eyes. "Yes, Cynical Sloan, I really mean it."

She bit her lip like she was trying not to smile. "Don't call me that."

"If the shoe fits."

"I ... accept your apology. I, too"—she cleared her throat—"am sorry. I didn't mean to make the situation worse by saying we were almost engaged."

I nodded. "Thank you. I appreciate that." I leaned forward again. "Do you think that maybe we can start over? Instead of me blackmailing you, we can move forward as one friend helping another friend out?"

Sloan took a deep breath. "I suppose we can do that."

I grinned. "Great."

Sloan looked down at her notebook again. She was trying to hide it, but I could see she was smiling, too.

"Let's get back to house details. And, while I have my paper out, maybe you should tell me what I'm going to need for the lake."

TEN

SLOAN

CALEB and I drove down a modest-sized driveway to a beautiful log house. It wasn't large, but it was gorgeous.

I leaned forward to get a better view out the front window. "This is a lake cabin?" I whistled. "No wonder you want to buy the store. You'd be rich. This is bigger than my house. My one and only house. I feel like we're on an episode of *House Hunters*." I raised my voice and said, *"Yes, we're looking for a second home on the beach, but we only have one million to spend, so our budget is a little tight."*

Caleb laughed. "It's not all the store. Ted was in finance before he quit to buy the store. He doesn't talk about it much. Just that it was stressful and he needed a change of pace, but I assume he made good money doing it. Also, Mary worked for the post office, so two incomes paid for this thing."

"Still, it's very impressive." I looked at Caleb. "They don't have any children, right?"

"Right."

"Do you think they'd adopt me?"

Caleb laughed. "Don't you have parents?"

"Yeah. But they don't have a lake *house*—emphasis on *house* because this is not a cabin. I mean, look at that wraparound porch. I want to retire here."

Caleb parked, and we got out of his vehicle. We both grabbed our bags from the backseat. I'd packed my swimsuit and an extra pair of clothes just in case. I didn't know how dirty we'd get out at the lake.

We walked up the porch stairs just as the front door opened, and Mary came out. "Hey, you two."

"Hi, Mary," I said.

Caleb kissed her on the cheek. "Hey, Mar."

"How was the drive?"

"Pretty good," I answered. "Not much traffic."

"Well, come in. I was just setting out some snacks for your arrival. Ted's down by the water. He'll be back up here soon."

I looked behind me to see the water was a nice distance away, probably a couple hundred feet.

We walked into the house, and of course, the inside was as beautiful as the outside.

I did a three-sixty with my mouth open in amazement. "How do you not live here year-round? It's so beautiful."

"We're actually thinking about it once Ted retires. Right now, it's too far to drive to the store every day."

"Oh, yeah, that pesky work thing," I said.

Mary laughed. "Speaking of work, how is house-hunting going?"

"Meh. Caleb is kind of picky."

Mary looked at Caleb. "You?"

"I'm not picky. It's just that, if I'm going to buy a house,

I'm going to buy something I really like." He made a *come here* motion. "Give me your bag. I'll put it in the guest bedroom."

"Thanks." I handed it over.

Caleb headed down the hall, and Mary and I went into the open kitchen. The kitchen and living room were basically all one big room, and I loved it. It made the area look wide and open.

"So, is Caleb really that picky?"

I sat down on the stool at the kitchen island. "Nah. I just like teasing him. I've had some clients that were real pains in my as—butt. Caleb is actually pretty easy. He hasn't really liked anything, but he doesn't complain."

"You know, I read something about couples who tease each other are happier." Mary pushed the veggie tray she'd laid out toward me. "Eat some."

"That's, uh … interesting," I replied because I had no idea what else to say. I quickly picked up a carrot, dipped it in some ranch, and shoved it in my mouth, so I wouldn't have to say another word.

"Ted's down by the water?" Caleb said from behind me.

I turned around, and the sight of Caleb in his swimming shorts and no shirt caused the carrot to fly into the back of my throat.

The man was gorgeous. Muscular but not too much with a light dusting of chest hair. I liked chest hair. And I caught a glimpse of at least one tattoo. I liked tattoos, too.

I pounded on my chest a couple of times, and thank God no one noticed.

Mary was already walking around to my side. "Yes, he's out there."

She opened the door and hollered out Ted's name just as I got the annoying slice of vegetable to the front of my mouth again.

"That's okay," Caleb said to Mary. "I'll walk down there." He looked at me. "Your stuff is in the spare bedroom if you want to change." His forehead crinkled. "Are you okay? Your face is kind of red."

"I'm fine." I stood. "Is it okay if I get a glass of water?"

"Oh, yes. Let me get you one," Mary said.

"That's okay. I can get it," I said quickly. I didn't want to look at Caleb's droolworthy body any more than I had to. It was making me want things I hadn't had in a long time. Like sex.

"It's probably time we head down to the water," Mary said. "After all, it's why you came here."

Mary and I had sat and talked for a good half hour. I really liked her, and we clicked, so finding things to converse about was easy. And I supposed I couldn't avoid seeing Caleb any longer.

It wasn't like I hadn't seen any attractive guys in the last two years just because I hadn't had a boyfriend or been physical with anyone, but I hadn't been pretending to be in a relationship with any of them.

I didn't know how I was going to be close to him, touch him, and kiss him without my hormones rising up and protesting. I had two trusty vibrators at home in my bedside drawer, but my body ... well, that bitch missed having a real man with a real penis sometimes. It was going to be hard to shut her up.

"… it's going to be in the low nineties today."

"I'm sorry," I said. "I was thinking. What did you say?"

Mary smiled. "I was saying, we should put on our swimsuits. It's already in the low eighties outside, and it's going to be in the low nineties today."

"Yeah, I saw that. It's a good day to be down by the water."

"Why don't you go change, and we'll walk down together?"

"Okay."

"Bedroom on the left is the guest room." Mary pointed down the hall.

I found the room easily enough and pulled out my stuff. I'd worn a sundress today so that I could pull it on and off over my suit. I'd be able to be covered up as long as possible, but if I wanted to get in the water, I'd eventually have to take my dress off.

As I pulled out my suit, the thought of Caleb seeing me in it made me want to shove it back inside my bag. It was probably as unsexy as any swimming suit could get and still be a swimming suit. It was a plain black two-piece, but the top was long enough to touch the bottoms. I probably would have brought a one-piece, but I hated getting naked just to pee. I'd bought the suit for efficiency, not to look good, and I hadn't thought twice as I threw it in my bag this morning.

But, after seeing Caleb looking all sexy, it was making me regret my decision.

I made a sound of disgust. *Who cares what Caleb thinks? You*

73

don't even like him like that, dummy. Ignore the hormones. Men suck, remember?

I took a deep breath and listened to my brain.

It didn't matter what I looked like in my suit. In fact, plain was probably better. Caleb and I weren't really involved, and I didn't want to be.

Right?

Right.

ELEVEN
CALEB

I LOOKED up from the Adirondack chair I was relaxing on when I heard Sloan and Mary walking down to the water.

My first reaction was disappointment. "Why aren't you in your suit?" I asked Sloan and pointed to the end of the long dock. "We got the boat and Jet Ski out."

Mary sat next to Ted while Sloan pulled the strap of her dress off one shoulder. "I'm wearing it underneath."

"Oh, good." I looked down at her other hand. "What do you have there?"

"Sunblock." She held out a fair-skinned arm. "I don't tan. I only burn."

My chair had a pullout ottoman attached. I patted it. "Sit. I'll get your back."

"Uh ..."

I raised my brow, hoping to communicate that it would be weird for her to not let her fiancé put sunblock on her. Ted and Mary were talking about food or something, but they were going to notice if Sloan turned down my offer.

When she didn't make a move, I rolled my eyes. I wasn't going to do anything inappropriate.

She sighed and sat down between my legs.

"Give me the bottle."

She squeezed some into her hands and gave it to me. I did the same with the sunblock. Sloan was already putting a good-sized amount on her legs, so I waited until she was done.

When she sat up, I put my hands on the tops of her shoulders.

She shivered.

"Sorry. Is it cold?"

"A little. I wasn't expecting it, I guess."

I returned to my sunblock job and brushed it all over her back, shoulders, and the back of her neck. Her hair was up in a ponytail, and I didn't want her to get burned. As my hands rubbed across her skin, I noticed how smooth it was, and that was when I knew my job was done. My swim trunks were starting to fit a little too tight, and I couldn't be thinking about her like that.

I dropped my hands and sat back in my seat. "All done."

She looked over her shoulder at me and smiled. A real, genuine smile. "Thank you."

Her sincere gratitude made me feel funny, and I didn't like it. I cleared my throat. "You're welcome."

As if she could sense my misery and wanted me to suffer more, she leaned back against me. I could feel her whole body against mine, and I froze underneath her.

She pulled her phone from the pocket of her dress. I could see what she was doing, and while she didn't make any attempt to hide it, I looked away to give her privacy.

A few seconds later, she elbowed me, so I looked down.

She had opened up her messages and typed something in the box but hadn't hit Send.

Relax. I'm your girlfriend, remember?

She was right, and I commanded my muscles to loosen.

She repeatedly hit the back button to erase what she'd written. As she did that, I looked up to see that the name she was under was Lover. She hadn't changed the name I had put on her phone, and I couldn't help but grin.

"What's so funny?" Ted asked.

I shook my head. "Nothing. Just the name Sloan has for me in her phone." I looked up at Ted and Mary. "What's for lunch?" I asked, changing the subject.

"I'm going to bring the portable grill down here," Ted said. "I was thinking hot dogs and brats for lunch. Burgers for dinner."

"And then we're going to build a fire in the pit and make s'mores," Mary added.

"Yum. I haven't had s'mores in forever," Sloan said.

I looked down at her as a message popped up on her screen from someone named Sydney.

> Sydney: Bear went into my purse again and ate my ChapStick! I had it hidden in a pocket, and I put my purse up on the shelf. And he still got it!

Sloan chuckled, and Ted said, "Now, this one's laughing, too."

She looked up. "I'm sorry. My sister-in-law is watching

my dog today, and he always finds her ChapStick when she dog-sits. It's become something of a joke."

That's right. I had already forgotten her sister-in-law was named Sydney. I did make sure to remember her brother's name was Travis, though, in case that came up in conversation.

"Caleb, you didn't tell us Sloan had a dog. She could have brought him here for the day."

Because I didn't know.

Apparently, we'd forgotten to discuss pets at our getting-to-know-each-other meeting.

"Uh ..."

"It's okay," Sloan said as she closed out of her messages and opened up her photos. "He's a Newfoundland-mix dog, so he takes up a lot of room in the truck." She started flipping through a bunch of photos of a big brown dog.

"Yeah," I added. "His name is Bear because he looks like one."

"He would love it, but it's much more relaxing, not bringing him," Sloan said.

"What's he mixed with?" Ted asked.

"His mom was a Newfoundland, and his dad was a fence-hopper." Sloan chuckled. "The owners are breeders and were a little surprised to find out their female was pregnant before she was supposed to be. I was more than happy to take one of the mutts off their hands."

"Next time, you'll have to bring him," Mary said. "We'd love to meet him."

Maybe I needed to rethink the five-date deal. On the first, we had gotten engaged. Now, on the second, they wanted to meet her dog. I could only imagine how much deeper this facade was going to get.

I nudged Sloan, and she sat up.

"Time to get on the Jet Ski," I said when she looked at me to see why I'd made her move.

She jumped up from the chair. "I'm driving."

I slowly rose from my seat and looked down at her. "You're dreaming, sweetheart. When I'm on the Jet Ski, I drive."

Sloan pulled her dress over her head and looked at Ted. "Where are the keys?"

"In the ignition," I heard Ted say, but I wasn't looking at him.

I was admiring Sloan's long, pale legs. For someone not that tall, she sure had a set on her. She also had a cute little bubble butt. Somehow, I had missed that.

She looked up at me and grinned, and I quickly moved my eyes from her body to her face.

"I'll race you. Whoever gets there first gets to drive," she said and sprinted toward the dock.

"Hey," I called out and went after her. I knew, if I wanted to, I could beat her, but at the last second, I decided to let her win.

She hopped on the Jet Ski and turned the engine over. "What do you say, Stanton? Are you man enough to let a woman drive?"

I went over to the boat, grabbed two life jackets, and threw one to her.

I put mine on and walked back over to her. "You don't scare me, Zehler."

She scooted forward and nodded toward the back. "Then, get on."

"Okay," I said. I untied the Jet Ski from the dock and got onto the back. "But I have to warn you, adrenaline gives me a hard-on."

Sloan laughed. "Now, you're trying to scare me." She pushed her ass back into me. "But it's not going to work." She revved the engine. "Hang on, big boy."

I put my arms around her as she took off.

TWELVE
SLOAN

I FLUNG my life jacket off. "Oh my God. I could feel your erection the entire time."

Caleb laughed as he removed his own life jacket. "I warned you." He took both the preservers and set them in the boat to dry. "You thought I was trying to scare you, but I was only speaking the truth."

We headed back up to the empty beach.

"I suppose this is my fault then?"

He shrugged. "You were the one going fast and doing all the crazy moves."

"I was not doing crazy moves. I was just having fun," I said defensively.

"Whatever you say. I thought maybe we were going to die out there. Hence, the erection."

"You're a jerk," I told him and pushed him away from me.

I'd kind of forgotten that we were on a narrow dock, and almost in slow motion, I watched Caleb's arms flail before he tumbled into the water.

I put my hand over my mouth in shock, and then I burst out laughing. "Oh my God. That was awesome."

Caleb stood up, unamused, and slicked his hair out of his face.

The water was a tad above his waist, and the sun glinted off the drops of water on him. He looked like a marine god rising from the sea. I felt a betraying tingle between my legs as I remembered his very impressive hard-on poking me in the butt.

At that moment, I admitted to myself that I'd purposely gone out of my way to do fancy moves. Some to impress Caleb and some to keep feeling his erection. It had been a long time since I felt one, and I kind of missed being close to a real-life one.

"I swear, I didn't push you in on purpose," I told him.

"You didn't push me on purpose?" he said, his voice full of doubt.

"I pushed you, yes, but I didn't mean for you to go in."

Despite the time on the Jet Ski, the top halves of us were pretty dry, and I could understand Caleb's dismay. I didn't want to get wet either.

I put my hand out. "Come on, I'll help you up."

He stalked toward me, and I yanked my arm back.

"Wait. Are you going to pull me in with you?"

"No. I'm not a child," he said.

"Okay." I tentatively put my hand back out to him. "I'm trusting you."

He grasped it in his hand. "Well, that was dumb of you." And he jerked me forward.

I screamed all the way down but quickly locked my lips

closed before I ended up with a mouthful of lake water going down my throat.

Caleb still had his hand clasped with mine and hauled me up. But only after I was good and wet.

I gasped and wiped the water out of my face. "You said you weren't going to pull me in," I accused him.

He grinned. "I lied." He let go of my hand. "That's what you get for pushing me in."

"Oh, you," I said and jumped on top of him.

I tried to push him back under the water, but he just laughed, not budging an inch.

Caleb wrapped his arms around me, pulling me tightly to his body. "You'd better be careful. You mess with the bull; you get the horns." He arched his brow. "Do you want to go under the water again?"

I wiggled against him. "No."

His smile fell, and his gaze went to my mouth. "What is it about you that makes me so hard?"

A soft gasp escaped my lips as his mouth lowered to mine.

He groaned and slid a hand up to cup the back of my neck.

I wrapped my arms around his neck and kissed him back. I hadn't gone as long not kissing a man as I had without sex, but it had been a while, and the last person hadn't really done much for me.

Not like Caleb.

I twisted around and tried to rub myself against his dick. It was a brand against my belly, and I wanted it between my thighs.

Caleb picked me up, and my legs went around his waist.

My mouth left his, and I kissed my way down his neck and onto his shoulder. I immediately regretted my decision to be in his arms because, now, my lips couldn't go any lower. I wanted to taste him all over.

He grabbed on to my ponytail and drew my head away from him. "Holy shit, you sure are full of surprises, baby."

I ignored him and went for his mouth again. Talking was overrated. I wanted more kissing. I wanted more of everything I knew Caleb could give me.

All it would take was one pull of his swim trunks and one yank of my suit to the side, and he could be inside me.

I groaned at the thought and rubbed my cleft over his cock.

"*Ca-leb. Slo-oan,*" a singsong voice called out.

It was Mary, and just like that, I was knocked back into my rational senses.

I jumped down from Caleb's body and turned away from him, embarrassed.

I'd been like a starving woman. No, I'd been like a woman on a liquid diet who had suddenly given herself permission to eat again.

I had actually been thinking about having sex. With Caleb. Outside. At someone else's home. I needed to clear my head.

Mary appeared at the dock. "There you two are. I saw the Jet Ski and wondered where you'd gone off to." She tilted her head. "Did you decide to go swimming?"

"Something like that," Caleb muttered.

"I pushed him in, and he pulled me in after him."

Mary pursed her lips. "That's not very nice, Caleb. Gentlemen don't pull ladies into the water."

She and Ted definitely treated Caleb like a son sometimes, and I had to grin.

"She pushed me in first," he mumbled.

"What was that?" Mary asked, like she knew he was mouthing off.

"Nothing," Caleb called back.

I tried not to laugh at him getting chided, but it was hard to resist.

"Come on in, you two," Mary said. "We're going to start lunch soon. You can help bring the stuff down, so we can eat." She turned and went back up to the house.

"Okay," I said and headed toward land. When I didn't hear anything behind me, I swung around. "Aren't you coming?"

Caleb shook his head. "I think I'll stay here another minute or two."

He looked down, and I realized that he didn't want Mary to see his erection.

I giggled, and his head snapped up.

He narrowed his eyes. "It's not funny."

"It's a little funny."

"You're lucky I really am a gentleman, or I'd drown you right now."

I snickered. "You'd have to catch me first." I spun around and sprinted toward the beach. I turned and finger-waved over my shoulder. "See you in a few minutes."

He flipped me the bird, and I laughed all the way up to the house.

THIRTEEN
CALEB

I STEWED in my sexual misery for about five minutes before I followed Sloan up to the house. I was still processing what had happened in the water as I walked up there.

She'd been like a wildcat the moment I kissed her. I hadn't planned on making a move on her. She looked so determined and cute that I couldn't help myself. The moment my lips touched hers, I was prepared for her to knee me in the balls.

Instead, she practically jumped me, rubbed her body against mine, and kissed me like she was running out of air and I was her next breath. I felt the heat of her pussy through the wetness of our suits, and pretty soon, I pictured her long, pale legs straddling me as she rode my cock. Hell, I thought she would have let me fuck her right then and there if I had tried.

I blew out a breath and stopped to adjust my trunks again. I needed to stop thinking about her, or I was going to walk into the house with an embarrassing hard-on. I looked up at the sky and pictured Mary's horror at seeing such a thing. My erection slowly went down. It was time to stop thinking about Sloan.

———

Lunch went well. I thought it might have been a little awkward between Sloan and me, but if I hadn't been standing in the water earlier with her body glued to mine, I would have never thought anything had happened. She either dismissed everything that had happened between us or she was an excellent actress. Either way, it was better for everyone even if it grated my nerves a little to see her so unaffected.

After lunch, the four of us went out on the boat and did a little waterskiing. I should say, Sloan and I did some water-skiing. Mary and Ted stayed in the boat.

By the time we got back to shore, it was almost time for dinner. We unloaded from the boat and headed up to the house.

"I'm going to sleep like the dead tonight," Sloan said.

"Agreed." I was already feeling the effects of the day wear on me, and the thought of driving home when I'd rather sit and relax weighed on my mind. I considered telling Sloan I wanted to leave now rather than later.

"I'm also starving. I think I'm going to eat four burgers for dinner."

Mary laughed. "I don't know if we have enough beef for that."

Sloan smiled. "How about two then?"

"I think we can manage," Mary said.

"Do you need help putting the boat and Jet Ski away?" I

asked Ted. "Otherwise, I was thinking of using your shower."

"I'm going to leave it out overnight. Mary and I will go out on it tomorrow. I'll put the Jet Ski away in a bit. Unless you want to use it again?"

I put up my hand. "No. I'm done with water for the day. I just want to take a shower and then be dry again."

"Could I get in on one of those, too?" Sloan said.

I grinned. "You're more than welcome to join me."

Sloan blushed.

Mary noticed Sloan's red cheeks. "Caleb, leave the poor girl alone." She turned to Sloan. "You can use the bathroom in our bedroom while Caleb uses the one in the hall."

"Thank you," Sloan told Mary. She stuck her tongue out at me as she walked past me into the house.

"You know, I was telling Sloan that couples who tease each other are happier," Mary said.

"Oh, yeah?"

Ted put his arm around Mary. "Does this mean, we're not happy?"

Mary patted his hand. "Of course not, dear. I was simply thinking how perfect Sloan is for Caleb."

I awkwardly scratched the back of my neck. "You think so, huh?"

"I do," Mary said.

"I agree," Ted said. "When you told me you had a girl-friend, I thought for sure you were feeding me a line of bull-shit. But I like her. And I think she's good for you."

"Well, thanks."

Ted slapped me on the arm. "You picked a good one."

He hugged Mary closer. "Come on, Mary. Let's go get those hamburgers started."

The two walked into the house with me lagging behind them as guilt began to descend on me.

I was lying to two people I loved and respected. When this whole thing had started, I'd justified it to myself because I wanted the store for good and honorable reasons. But lying to get it wasn't honorable, and I felt like a fraud.

Sloan and I ran into each other in the hall after our showers. She was wearing shorts and a cute little T-shirt, and I tried to think about her instead of my guilt.

"Uh-oh," she said. "What's wrong?"

"Why would you say something's wrong?"

"You look like you just ran over someone's dog," she whispered. "What gives?"

I sighed and pulled her into the spare bedroom. "I feel guilty."

Realization crossed her face. "I appreciate it, but you don't have to feel bad. While I don't want to, I admit that I kissed you back."

I frowned. "What? No. I don't feel guilty about that. It's probably not something we should have been doing, but I don't feel guilty."

"Oh. Then, what do you feel bad about?"

"For lying to Ted and Mary."

"Oh," she said sympathetically.

"After you went into the house, they told me that they think you're good for me and that I picked a good one."

Sloan beamed. "They like me."

"Of course they like you. What's not to like?" I looked down at my feet. "But all their praise made me realize that lying to them is wrong. Even if I'm doing it for a semi-good reason." I looked up at her. "I think I should tell them."

Sloan took a step toward me. "No."

"No? I thought you'd be all for it. You'd get out of any more dates with me."

She shook her head. "Telling them now will only make *you* feel better. They will feel awful, and you're certain to lose any chance of buying the store. Do you really want that other guy to have it?"

I shook my head. "No."

"So, don't tell them. We'll finish our last three dates, and then we'll break up. They never have to know, and no one gets hurt."

"Are you sure that's the right thing to do?"

She put her hand on my arm. "I'm positive."

"Does this mean, you'll make out with me some more?"

Sloan pushed me away. "Not on your life."

I put my arm around her shoulders and led her out to the hall. "You really are a good fake girlfriend."

"Thanks. You're not too bad yourself."

"I'll take that as a *maybe* on making out again."

FOURTEEN
SLOAN

I PULLED my marshmallow from the fire. "Perfect."

"Here you go, dear," Mary said, handing me a paper plate with chocolate and graham crackers on it.

"Thank you," I told her and quickly stuck my marshmallow on top of the chocolate bar and in between the graham crackers before it cooled off. My first bite reminded me of what I'd been missing. "I need to have these more often."

"They're the perfect way to end the day," Ted said.

"Sloan."

I looked over at Caleb. He was smiling at me.

"What?"

He pointed to the corner of his mouth. "You have a little bit of chocolate right there."

I used my finger to swipe up the runaway dessert. I'd also forgotten how messy they were. I looked at Caleb. "Better?"

"Yep." He took his own bite, and the same thing happened to him.

I laughed. "Now, you have some on your chin."

"Oh jeez," he said. He tried to wipe it off and missed.

"Come here," I told him.

He leaned toward me, and I got the string of chocolate off his face. I lifted my thumb to show him how much had been on there.

He took my hand in his. "Wow. Did I even get any in my mouth?"

I laughed.

Caleb smiled and sucked the chocolate off my thumb. He did it very casually, not sexual in the least.

It still made me shiver and suck in a breath.

He let go of my hand. "You okay?" He looked up at the sky. "The sun is almost set. Are you cold?"

"It can get chilly down here by the water at night," Mary said.

"I'm okay. I didn't even think to bring a sweatshirt since it was so warm this morning."

Caleb stood and handed me his plate. "Can you hold this for a sec? I don't want it to blow away."

"Sure."

Caleb took off for the house, and I leaned back on my chair and rubbed my arms. Despite the cold, I was still enjoying myself. It was so peaceful out.

A few minutes later, I heard the sound of Caleb returning. My back was to him since I was facing the water, so I was surprised when he set a sweatshirt on my lap.

"Here you go."

I sat up with surprise. "Is this yours?"

"Yeah. I thought I had it in my truck, so I went to check."

I really wanted to put it on, but I held it out to him. "Are you sure you don't want it? What if you get cold?"

Caleb chuckled. "I'll be fine. You put it on."

"Thank you," I said and quickly pulled it over my head before he changed his mind. It was nice and big and soft on the inside. Even better, it smelled like him. Something else I missed. The smell of a man.

"I don't think I've ever seen you wear a sweatshirt, Caleb," Mary said.

"That's because I don't. Not even in winter," he said.

My brain perked up at this. This seemed like something a significant other would know, and I hoped I hadn't messed up by asking him if he wanted the sweatshirt. "I do tease him that sleeping next to him is like a furnace," I said. "I never understand how someone who gives off so much heat has any left in their body."

Caleb grinned and pulled his T-shirt away from his chest in a back-and-forth motion. "What can I say? I'm hot."

Everyone laughed, and my possible blunder was forgotten.

Caleb patted his chair. "Come over here. Let me give you some of my heat."

I didn't know if it was a good idea after our kiss, but we were in front of Ted and Mary, so I got up and moved to his chair. His had a place for us to stretch out our legs. Caleb pulled me back against him and enveloped me in his arms.

I didn't fight him or my own body. I'd had a fun day, but I'd burned a lot of energy, and I deserved to relax.

"So, when are you going to buy this girl a ring, Caleb?" Mary said.

I held up my left hand. "Yeah, Caleb, when are you going to buy me a ring?"

"I can't afford her," he said. "She told me she wants at least three carats."

I rolled my eyes even though Ted and Mary probably couldn't see me. "I do not. I just want something small. I've always dreamed of having a princess solitaire with mine and my fiancé's birthstones on each side in a smaller size. I don't need big, but I want it to be unique to the two of us."

"That's so sweet," Mary said. "When is your birthday?"

"I'm February, so my birthstone is amethyst. Caleb's is a pink stone or an opal, but I vote for the pink stone. My engagement ring will be very girlie."

"But unique," Mary added.

"But unique," I agreed. "But we aren't *officially* engaged yet. We've only been talking about it."

"Well, when are you going to ask the girl?" Ted said.

"When the time is right, I suppose," said Caleb. "I want it to be special."

The conversation turned to something else, and I let my eyes drift closed. With the fire warming my feet and legs and Caleb warming the rest of my body, I was feeling pretty comfortable. The sound of his chest rumbling under my ear was lulling me to sleep.

"Are you sure you don't want to stay the night?" Mary asked. "I think Sloan is almost asleep."

I smiled. "I'm awake. Just relaxing over here."

"Would you like to stay? That's what the spare room is for."

I didn't answer right away, and after a few seconds, Caleb said, "It's up to Sloan."

It was tempting even if I had to sleep in the same bed as him, but it wasn't a good idea. "I probably shouldn't. I have to get home to my dog," I said.

"When do you want to leave?" Caleb asked.

"I don't. Kidding. A half hour or so? Let me just lie here a little longer."

"Okay." He kissed me on top of my head, and I closed my eyes.

FIFTEEN
CALEB

"YOUR GIRL'S OUT," Ted said.

I looked down at Sloan to see she was indeed asleep. "Crap," I whispered loudly, so Mary and Ted could still hear me. "What do I do now? I suppose I could carry her to the truck."

"Don't do that," Mary said. "Just lay her down in the guest bedroom and stay the night. You two can go home in the morning."

"I don't know," I said. Sloan might not appreciate me bunking next to her, but I certainly couldn't sleep anywhere else. We'd literally been talking about engagement rings an hour earlier. "Maybe I should head home now."

Immediately after I spoke, I yawned so hard that my jaw hurt. I was beat.

"Caleb, don't be silly. You are tuckered out. Go to bed," Mary said.

It was too appealing to pass up. The thought of driving home with no one to talk to sounded horrible. I didn't know if I'd be able to stay awake.

"It's not safe," Ted said. "What if you fall asleep at the wheel?"

I put my head against the back of the chair and closed my eyes. "I was thinking the same thing."

"Caleb."

I opened my eyes and lifted my head. "What?"

Ted was laughing. "Go to bed. You just fell asleep on us."

"Okay," I said, giving in without much of a fight.

It took some maneuvering, but I slipped out from behind Sloan, so I could stand, and then I picked her up. She shifted in my arms but stayed asleep.

I carried her into the almost-dark house. The sun had set a while ago, and the only light on was the one above the stove. I cautiously made my way to the bedroom, not wanting to hit her head on the wall because I couldn't see well.

In the bedroom, our bags were on the bed, so I had to use one leg to kick them off before anyone could lie down. At the rate I was going, my adrenaline was going to start pumping and wake me up. I'd be ready to drive home, and I would have carried her to bed for nothing.

I also kicked down the covers enough that I wouldn't wake her by trying to pull them out from underneath her.

When I was finally ready, I bent over and carefully set her on the bed.

And that was when she woke up.

She wrapped her arms around my neck, so I couldn't stand up.

"Caleb?" Her voice was sleepy, and I realized she wasn't fully awake.

"Yeah, baby?"

"Am I in bed?"

"Yeah. Is that okay?"

"Mmm…yeah. I'm tired."

"Is it okay if I lie down next to you? I'm tired, too."

"Sure." She rubbed her nose against my neck. "You smell good, and you're warm."

I chuckled. "That's good. I think."

Her breathing deepened, so I reached behind me and removed her arms from around me. I took off her shoes and tucked her under the covers.

I kicked off my own shoes and was about to get into bed when I remembered Sloan had said something about her dog.

Crap.

I pulled the covers down just enough to pat her down for a phone. Thankfully, it was in her pocket on her side that was lying up. I took it out and pressed home.

It needed a fingerprint.

I took her hand and opened it as I shook my head. Some security option this was.

I found Sydney in her messages and sent a quick text, pretending to be her. I didn't know what she'd said about me, and I didn't want to put Sloan in an awkward position.

> Me: Can you watch Bear overnight? I'm too tired to drive home.

I closed my eyes and willed her sister-in-law to message me right away, so I didn't have to stand forever, waiting. Her phone buzzed, and I opened my eyes.

Sydney: Sure. No problem. I'll make Travis take care of him.

I thanked her and put the phone down on the table next to Sloan's side of the bed. I walked around to the other side, and I fell asleep a minute after my head hit the pillow.

I woke up the next morning when someone slapped my ass.

"Wake up, Caleb."

I lifted my head and blinked away the sleep. "Huh?"

Sloan was sitting up in bed. "We need to go home."

I let my head drop back down. "Five more minutes."

She smacked my butt again and laughed. "No. We need to get up. I forgot about my dog."

"Your sister-in-law is watching him," I said into the pillow.

"I know. But she expected me home last night."

"It's taken care of. I texted her to say you weren't coming home."

"What? I can't understand you."

I lifted my head just enough to say, "Check your messages." I closed my eyes again and was almost—this close—asleep again when Sloan hugged me.

"You messaged Sydney for me. Thank you."

I groaned and flung her off my back. "Fine, I'm up. We can go home." I rolled over and sat on the edge of the bed.

"Oh, no rush. Now that I know Bear's taken care of, you can go back to sleep."

I looked over my shoulder and glared at her. "I hate you right now."

Sloan laughed. "Someone's cranky in the morning."

"And someone is way too goddamn cheery."

Sloan laughed again.

Mary made the two of us a big breakfast and wouldn't let us leave until we ate. We finally got on the road around ten in the morning.

It was about a half hour into the drive when I realized that neither of us had said anything, but it wasn't odd.

It seemed that Sloan and I were getting comfortable with each other.

I looked over at her. "Do you think that, once this is all over, you and I will stay friends?"

She looked at me. "I have no idea." She tilted her head. "Would it be weird if we broke up and stayed friends?"

"No. I'm friends with some of my exes. Aren't you?"

She curled up her lip. "Not even close."

I reached over and put my hand on hers. "I think I would like it if we were. I had fun this weekend. I'm glad you were there."

Sloan smiled at me. "I had fun, too."

For a second, I thought maybe we would actually become more than friends, but her phone beeped, and the moment was gone.

Sloan pulled her hand away and looked at her cell. "Uh-oh."

"What?"

"Mel asked me to come and pick her up at your brother's."

Sloan's phone beeped two more times.

"Right now." She drew in a quick breath. "Something happened with Neil." She looked up at me. "It doesn't sound like it's going well. She locked herself in the bathroom."

"We'll go there right away. Tell her we're coming."

I pushed down on the gas and hoped my brother wasn't going to do anything stupid.

SIXTEEN

SLOAN

> Me: What sparked this fight? Why are you in the bathroom?

> Melanie: Because I can't even look at him right now.

> Me: Can't you leave?

> Melanie: He has my car keys.

"THAT DICK," I muttered.

"What happened?" Caleb asked from the driver's seat.

"Your fucking brother has her car keys and won't let her leave."

Caleb's hand tightened on the steering wheel. "Asshole. Melanie is too good for him."

I appreciated Caleb saying this. Some families were so loyal that they were blind to each other's faults.

I turned back to my phone.

Me: I knew you should have broken up with him last weekend. I'm sorry I made you wait.

Melanie: We were right to wait. He would have totally suspected it was me who'd ruined his paint job. I just wish we had pranked him a month ago, so he was already out of my life.

Me: Why? You still haven't told me what sparked the fight.

Melanie: I don't want to tell you. It's embarrassing.

Me: Mel, we've been friends for a long time. You can tell me anything.

Melanie: I went to use Neil's computer. There was a letter sitting on his desk. It was from the clinic.

Melanie: He tested positive for an STI, and now, I have to get tested, too.

"*Motherfucker.*"

"What? What's wrong?" Caleb asked.

Me: What the actual fuck! Was he even going to tell you?

Melanie: He says he was, but the letter was dated on Monday. And it only takes a day or two to deliver in town. He had to have known for a few days.

"I'm going to kill him."

"What the hell happened, Sloan?"

I looked up at Caleb and debated on whether or not I should tell him. Melanie was embarrassed, and even though it wasn't her fault, I didn't want her to feel worse.

Caleb put his hand on my knee. "You can trust me."

"There's a strong chance your brother gave Melanie an STI."

Caleb's face morphed into anger. It was then I realized I had never seen him mad before. "I'm going to kill him. He just can't keep it in his pants, can he?"

"You're not going to kill him. I've already called dibs."

Caleb squeezed my knee. "We can do it together."

I looked down at my cell.

> Me: You have no reason to be embarrassed. Neil is a grade A dick. This is not your fault.

> Melanie: But I already knew he'd cheated on me.

> Me: Hon, the damage was probably already done. Besides, you told me you weren't having sex with him anymore.

> Melanie: Don't hate me. But I slipped last night. I'm not like you. I can't go years without sex. I knew I was breaking up with him. I wanted one last orgasm.

I gagged a little. I didn't think Neil was worth sleeping with even if he wasn't a cheater. The two of us obviously had different taste.

Me: Please tell me you used a condom.

Melanie: He would have been suspicious. We haven't used them for months.

I closed my eyes and counted to ten.

Me: I'll take you to the clinic on Monday morning myself, and we'll get you tested for everything we possibly can.

Melanie: The sheet says he only has gonorrhea.

Me: You're still getting tested for everything.

Melanie: Okay. You're right.

Melanie: I told him it's over, and now, he's pounding on the door, demanding I come out.

Me: Hold on a bit longer. I'll be there as soon as I can.

"Is there any way we can go faster?" I asked. "Neil's trying to break down the door."

———

Caleb pounded on his brother's door and opened it before Neil could answer. It was handy, having a family member around who could do that.

"Neil," Caleb called out. "Where are you?"

"In here," he called from the hallway.

When we got there, we saw Neil standing in front of the bathroom door.

"Move out of the way," Caleb said.

Neil pointed at the closed door. "She won't come out."

"Step away, Neil," Caleb said.

Neil scoffed and stepped back.

Caleb grabbed Neil's arm. "Let's go in here," he said and guided his brother toward the living room.

I knocked softly. "Mel? It's me. Can you open up?"

I heard the lock click, and the door opened a sliver.

Mel's eye peeked through. "Where is he?"

"In the living room with Caleb."

"Caleb?"

"Yeah. It's a long story. Can you open the door and come out?"

Melanie shook her head. "I don't know."

This didn't sound good. "Mel, has Neil ever hurt you before?"

I knew he was a slimy cheater, but I had never gotten the impression that he was an abuser.

"No."

"Then, why won't you come out?" I asked.

"Because I'm afraid I'll hurt him."

"That's my girl." I bit my bottom lip to keep myself from laughing, but a chuckle escaped anyway. "What if I promise to hold you back, so you don't go to jail for assault?"

She slowly opened the door. "Okay. But could you accidentally let me kick him in the nuts first?"

"I'll think about it. I'm pretty sure that's still assault."

"He cheated on me, Sloan, and gave me a disease. And he had to have known or suspected something, or he wouldn't have gotten tested."

I stepped forward and pulled her into my arms. "I know, hon. He doesn't deserve you. But try to remember his ruined car."

Mel pulled back and smiled at me. "That does make me feel better."

"What is wrong with you?" Caleb yelled from the living room. "Why do you manage to cheat on every girl you've ever dated?"

"Not every girl," Neil said.

"That's your defense? 'Not every girl'?"

Mel and I slowly walked into the living room.

"Mel, baby," Neil said when he saw her. He stepped forward. "I'm sorry."

Caleb and I moved to block him from her.

"Stay away from her," I said. "She wants nothing to do with you anymore."

Neil sneered at Melanie. "Whatever. You're not worth it anyway." He turned his eyes to me. "I should've picked you instead."

He'd said it to get a rise out of Melanie and me. What I didn't think Neil had expected was that his comment would affect his brother, too. Before anyone else could react, Caleb swung his fist forward and punched Neil in the face.

Blood spurted from his nose, and he brought his hands up to cup his face. "What the hell was that for? Jesus, are you fucking her?"

Caleb chose not to answer. "Ladies, I think it's time for

us to go."

"My keys," Melanie said.

Caleb held them up in his non-hitting hand. "I already got them."

I walked up to Neil. "I wouldn't sleep with you even if we were both wearing hazmat suits," I said low and calm right before I kneed him in the balls.

Neil dropped to his knees and moaned.

"That's for Melanie because she's totally worth it."

Caleb wrapped his hand around my bicep. "Come on. It's time to go."

Once outside, I grabbed my purse from Caleb's truck. "I'm going with Mel."

He nodded his head and stepped forward. He put his hand out but dropped it right away. "I'll talk to you later."

I wondered what he would have done if Melanie hadn't been standing there.

I got in her car, and we took off.

"Are you going to be okay?"

"Eventually."

"We can egg his house next," I offered jokingly.

She chuckled, but her heart wasn't in it. "That's okay. I want to stay far away from him."

"I don't blame you. But what about all your stuff?"

She groaned. "I don't want to think about it right now. Let's talk about something else."

"Okay. What?"

"Like, what are you doing with Caleb?"

"Would you believe, looking at houses?" I asked.

Mel gave me a look, and I laughed.

"I'm helping him out with something …" I started.

SEVENTEEN
CALEB

LATER THAT EVENING, I was doing some research on managing a business when there was a knock at my apartment door.

For a moment, I wondered if I'd ordered takeout and forgotten. I'd been thinking of calling up my favorite Chinese food place for the last hour or so, but I'd been too in the zone to stop reading and make the call.

I got up from my desk and went to the door. I was in basketball shorts and a button-up shirt. I'd left it open with nothing on underneath, so I grabbed the sides and pulled them together in my hand before answering the door.

It was Sloan.

"Oh. Hey," I said and let go of my shirt.

I watched how her eyes immediately went to my chest. I couldn't be sure, but I thought I'd seen her do that a few times yesterday, too.

"I came to get my stuff."

I stepped aside, so she could enter my apartment. "Your bag is in the living room."

"Thanks."

"How's Melanie?" I asked as I led Sloan to her stuff.

"A little freaked out about going to the doctor. But glad that she and Neil are over." She picked up her backpack from the floor and slung it over her shoulder. "And she was a little curious about what we were doing together."

"What did you tell her?" I hoped I hadn't put her in a bad spot with her friend.

"That you asked me to help you out and that we're kind of friends now. She still doesn't know that you know it was us who vandalized Neil's car."

"I'm sorry. I don't know who did that to my brother's car," I said, playing dumb.

Sloan smiled. "How's your hand?"

I lifted my arm and made a fist a couple of times. "A little sore but not bad." I smiled. "It feels a lot better than Neil's nose, I'm sure."

Sloan moved toward me. "Can I ask why you punched him?"

"Because he's an asshole."

The corner of Sloan's mouth tilted up. "I know. But you already knew that. What was it about his comment that made you do it?"

I looked away from her because I didn't want to tell her why. "Do I have to say?"

"Humor me."

I looked back down at her. "I didn't like what he said about you." I shrugged. "I guess, in my head, I'd started thinking of you as mine. And I didn't like the way he'd insulted you." I put my hand up. "Before you berate me for being a sexist pig, I already know it was very caveman of me to—"

Sloan dropped her bag and jumped me.

Our mouths slammed together in one of the hottest kisses of my life. Her hands were all over me. In my hair, on my face, on my neck, and down my chest.

I kissed her neck as she said, "Where's your bedroom?"

I lifted my head. "Are you sure that's a good idea?"

Please say yes, please say yes, I *and* my dick were thinking.

I put my mouth on her neck again and rubbed her pussy over my erection once before she told me no and walked out of my apartment. The good news was, it would only take me minutes to get myself off once she left; I was so horny.

"Caleb"—she pulled my hair, forcing me to look at her —"did you hear what I said?" She didn't wait for me to answer. "I said, I don't care if it's *not* a good idea. I want you inside me."

I kissed her long and hard. "I think you're trying to kill me."

She grinned. "Move it, Caleb, before I change my mind."

I raced toward my room and threw us both on the bed. We landed on our sides, but Sloan quickly pushed me onto my back. She spread her fingers out across my chest and nudged my shirt out of the way. Then, she practically ripped the sleeves, pulling it off my arms.

Wild Sloan was back, and I grew even harder.

She slid down my body until she was between my legs. I barely had time to lift my head to watch her pull down my shorts before she took my cock into her mouth.

My eyes rolled into the back of my head, and my hips

thrust involuntarily.

"Shit." I looked at her again. "I didn't mean to jerk like that. It just feels so—*ahhhhh*," I called out as she sucked so hard that her cheeks hollowed.

At the rate she was going, I didn't know how much longer I could last. I was going to come embarrassingly fast. She wasn't even stroking me or playing with my balls.

Her hands were roaming my body, like she was trying to touch every millimeter of skin within her reach.

But that was probably what I found so hot about it. She was into me; she was into my body. She wanted to touch me.

Her hands were caressing my chest as her forehead fell to my stomach, and I felt my shaft hit the back of her throat. She made a sound, much like the sound I'd heard her make the first time she tasted Mary's lasagna, as if my cock tasted *that good*.

And that was why it was over for me. "I'm going to—" I tried to warn her, but I couldn't manage to get all the words out before I exploded in her mouth.

I might have blacked out, I might have cried, I might have seen God. I didn't really know. All I did know was that it was the best damn orgasm I'd ever had.

Sloan crawled up my body and spread out on me, and I gave myself one minute of recovery time before I flipped her over.

She squeaked at the sudden movement and smiled.

"My turn," I told her. I kicked off my shorts, which had been hanging halfway on my legs, and pulled off her shirt. I got off the bed and pulled down her shorts and underwear as she took off her bra.

Starting with my hands at her ankles, I glided them up

her calves and shins, over her knees, and across her thighs. When I reached the apex, I looked her in the eyes and pushed her legs open.

I got down on my knees. I could smell her arousal as much as I could see it on her pink pussy. I couldn't wait to get inside her.

But it wasn't time yet.

Even though I could see her wetness, I slowly pushed my middle finger into her.

She sucked in a breath, and her inner muscles clamped down on me.

"Play with your nipples," I told her.

Her hands came up to her breasts as I used my thumb to seek out her clit.

She moaned, and I grinned at my find.

I pulled my hand away and put my mouth on her magic little button. I had no idea if Sloan would ever let me get intimate with her again, and I wanted to do everything I could with her before our time was over. Including eating her pretty pussy.

I put my mouth between her legs and gave her clit a small lick. She shivered, so I did it a bit more. I took my time, teasing her little nub until it was hard and throbbing against my tongue.

I pushed a finger back into her and added another, curling them until I found her G-spot. I was in it for the long haul. I wanted to make this woman come, but she put my quick trigger to shame.

I'd barely gotten to play at all when her thighs clamped around my head, and she screamed so hard that I was actually embarrassed my neighbors would hear.

I tried to cover her mouth, but I couldn't see what I was doing very well. My head was still between her legs, and while I needed her to be quiet, I wasn't going to cut off her orgasm. I wasn't going to stop until she pushed me away.

My fingers found her lips, and she grabbed my hand, sucking a couple of fingers into her mouth. My dick automatically remembered what it felt like to be inside her like that, and my hard-on went from halfway there to full mast again.

Sloan pushed my hand away from her face first. "Oh God, oh God, oh God," she chanted. Then, her legs fell to the sides, and she pushed the rest of me away. "I can't—" She took a deep breath. "I'm"—deep breath—"too sensitive."

This gave me a deep sense of satisfaction, and I reached for the drawer in my nightstand. I found a condom within seconds, and in less than fifteen more, it was covering me.

I stood up and climbed onto the bed beside her. I pulled Sloan's body against mine as I kissed her once again. I wanted her to taste herself on my tongue, as I could taste myself on hers.

When she began rubbing her lower body against me, I moved my mouth down to her breasts. Her nipple pebbled under my tongue, and she moaned as her fingers grabbed on to my hair.

I kissed my way back up to her ear. "Are you ready?" I whispered.

Her breathy, "Yes," was exactly what I'd wanted to hear.

I moved over her body and in between her legs. I lined up my cock at her entrance and pushed myself inside her.

EIGHTEEN
SLOAN

THE NEXT AFTERNOON, Melanie and I sat in the doctor's waiting room.

Mel was flipping through a magazine, but I could tell she wasn't even trying to find anything to read because she never even paused to scan the articles.

She slammed the magazine into her lap, making me jump in my seat. "What gives?" she said to me.

"What do you mean?" I asked.

"You haven't stopped fidgeting since we got here. If I didn't know that it was my doctor's appointment, I would assume it was yours from all the nervousness you're putting out there."

"I'm sorry. But I'm as worried about you as you are, you know," I told her. It was mostly the truth. I was also feeling sore from the amazing and unexpected sex I'd had last night.

But I didn't want to think about that.

"I know you are. And that's why you're my friend," Melanie said.

"How much longer do you think it's going to take?"

Melanie shrugged. "I don't know. It's only been five minutes. I'm sure they'll come and get me soon." She threw the magazine on the chair on the other side of her.

"Nothing good?"

"I can't concentrate. I'm trying to stay calm, but I'm nervous."

"Has Neil contacted you at all?" I asked.

"He sent me a text."

"*What?*" I had expected her to say no because she hadn't previously mentioned it. "Why?" I narrowed my eyes. "Does he want to get back together?"

"No. He told me I had until Wednesday to get my stuff out of his house, or he's throwing it all away."

"What a dick. When are you going to do that?"

"I already did."

"*Melanie.*"

"What?"

"That's two things you haven't told me today. I thought I was your best friend."

She laughed and grinned at me. "That dick forgot that I still had a key to his house. And, since I'd called into work today, I figured it was better to go when he wasn't there."

"Why didn't you call me? I could have squeezed you into my schedule today. I would have even rescheduled something for as important as that."

"I know you would have, but really, I was okay. It took me about fifteen minutes. I had already started taking my stuff home after I found out about the cheating." She hit her knee against mine. "Besides, if I took you with me, I was afraid you'd do something to his house."

I crossed my arms over my chest. "No, I wouldn't have. It would have been obvious it was you, and I wouldn't want you to get into trouble."

"You're such a liar. You wouldn't have been able to resist. You would have done something."

I would like to think I would have been able to control myself, but there was a chance I would have done something to get back at him. I dropped my arms. "You're probably right."

"Ha." She pointed a finger at me. "I knew it. And I didn't want Neil calling me up, pissed at me about something. I want to be done with him. I don't want to talk to him or think about him any more than I have to."

"I don't blame you."

"Now, I understand why you avoid men like the plague and don't date." She smiled. "At least, not for real. Your situation with Caleb is still a surprise to me."

I scowled. "I don't avoid men like the plague. Not dating is not the same as avoiding."

"Yeah, well, at least with fake dating, you don't have to worry about getting an infection. You have to have sex for that."

I looked to the door where the nurses and medical assistants came out and called names, hoping someone would call Melanie's name soon. I didn't want to have this conversation with her. "Yep."

"Yep?" I could see her following my gaze out of the corner of her eye. "Why are you staring at the door?" She gasped. "Sloan Zehler, you dirty dog."

I looked at Mel with wide eyes. "What?"

"That is the worst fake innocent look I've ever seen."

She leaned closer and lowered her voice. "You totally fucked Caleb, didn't you?"

I didn't say anything.

She narrowed her eyes. "You told me yesterday it was completely platonic." She looked me up and down. "And you weren't lying then, which means …"

"Which means you need to be quiet and stop talking about it," I said quickly.

Melanie grinned. "Which means you went to his place last night and got busy."

I turned away. "I'm not talking to you about this."

There were people all over the waiting room. None were close to us, but I still didn't want them to overhear.

"Was it good? Did he make you come?" She put her hand on my arm, causing me to look at her. "If he screws anything like his brother, he made you come."

"Shh," I hissed and looked around to make sure no one had heard. "Will you lower your voice, please?"

"I'll stop talking if you answer me." She clasped her hands together and stuck out her lower lip. "Please. I just broke up with my boyfriend, and I'm about to get tested for something you only get from having sex. This is the only thing that is making me happy right now."

"Fine. You're lucky I love you."

Mel grinned.

I looked around one more time and put my head so close to hers that we were almost touching. "Yes, okay? He made me come. A lot."

Caleb knew what he was doing in bed, and I hadn't been able to get enough. I had made myself leave while he was sleeping before I asked him for round two. This was why I hadn't had sex in the first place. It made me realize how much I missed it. And Caleb made me miss it real bad. So badly that I wanted to do it again.

Mel squealed and pumped her fist in the air.

I immediately pushed it down.

"Sloan got laid, Sloan got laid," she whispered in a singsong voice.

"Will you knock it off?" I said, trying not to laugh. "It happened once, and it's not going to happen again."

She stopped smiling. "Why the hell not?"

"Because it only complicates things."

"How many dates do you have left?"

"Three."

Melanie snorted. "You're absolutely going to bone him again."

"I will not."

"How much do you want to bet?" She wiggled her eyebrows.

"Five dollars."

She laughed. "Keep your money. I already know I've won. You wouldn't have bet so low unless you knew you were going to lose."

"Melanie," a voice said from across the room.

"Good luck," I told her. "I'll be here when you get out."

Melanie stood and took a deep breath, and I wanted to do something to distract her.

"Fifty bucks," I said.

"Huh?"

"I bet you fifty bucks I won't sleep with him again."

She smiled and turned around, so she could walk backward. "I'll start dreaming of ways I'm going to spend it. I've been eyeing a pair of shoes ..." She did a one-eighty and disappeared behind the wooden door.

I was glad I'd given her something to think about besides having an infection from her ex.

I, on the other hand, was determined not to lose the bet. I was not going to sleep with Caleb again.

NINETEEN
CALEB

"HEY, CALEB. I NEED YOUR HELP."

I'd been going around the store and picking things up. Customers constantly took things off shelves and didn't put them back.

Upon hearing my name, I turned to see Rick approaching me, and I groaned. This guy was my competition, and I didn't want to help him with anything. I wanted Ted to see that he wasn't the right fit for the store.

But I couldn't do that. "What is it?" I said in a short tone. I was going to help, but it didn't mean I had to like it.

He handed me a sheet. It was a list of our inventory. "I'm going through the list, but things aren't lining up. Some stuff is short, and some stuff is high."

I pointed to the top of the page. "This is from last month. Did you add the items that people had brought in and sold to us? And did you subtract this month's sales?"

Rick turned red, and I couldn't help but feel bad for him.

"Run the numbers against those two spreadsheets, and if you're still having problems, come talk to me."

"Okay." Rick turned away but then swung right back around. "Where do I find them?"

Unbelievable.

"In the file cabinet. In the office."

"Thanks," Rick said and headed to the back of the store.

I knew how to do all that stuff without even thinking about it, and Ted wanted to give the store to someone who had no idea what he was doing. I knew Rick wasn't dumb, but I also knew he wasn't ready to run the store. I hoped Ted realized that he would have to stay on for a few more months and do some training.

Shit.

Unless Ted expected me to train Rick.

Fuck that. If Ted even hinted at that, I was going to leave. I would respect Ted's decision, but it didn't mean I had to babysit the new owner.

I threw a couple of hats down on the shelf, not caring where they landed, and I knew that part of my frustration was the fact that, ever since Sloan and I'd had sex, she'd been ignoring me. Kind of. She was doing the grown-up version of ignoring me. All week, every time I sent her a text, she would reply in short, impersonal answers.

But she should know by now that I didn't give up very easy when I wanted something. And what I wanted was for her to stop avoiding me.

The following morning, I knocked on Sloan's door. Two seconds later, I heard the sound of a dog barking, and I knew it had to be Bear.

"I'm coming," Sloan yelled from inside the house. And then I heard her say, "Calm down, Bear," before the door opened.

Sloan's hair was up in a messy ponytail, her face appeared to be makeup-free, and she was in her pajamas.

"Good morning," I said cheerfully and shoved one of the two coffees I'd picked up on my way over to her house into her hand.

A big, furry brown head pushed its way between Sloan and the door, and I got down on my haunches.

"Hey there, big guy," I said, petting him with my free hand. "You must be Bear."

Bear licked my face.

"What are you doing here?" Sloan asked.

I stood up. Bear nudged my leg, wanting more pets. I ruffled his head one more time.

"Oh, I'm sorry," I said with fake sincerity. "I'm looking for"—I held up a finger and grabbed my phone to look at the screen—"a Sloan Zehler. She's supposed to be my realtor, but I haven't been able to get in touch with her all week."

Sloan rolled her eyes, turned around, and walked into her house. Since she hadn't closed the door in my face, I followed her in.

"Did you have to come so early?" she asked.

"It's eight in the morning on a Friday. I thought you'd be up and ready for work. Besides, I didn't want you to skip out on me if I told you I was coming."

"I go into the office when I want," she explained. "And I wouldn't have skipped out if you had told me you were coming over."

"Right," I said doubtfully.

"I wouldn't have," she said adamantly.

"You've been avoiding me."

"No. I've just been busy."

Since I still had my cell in my hands, I pulled up our text messages. "Hmm, let's see what my phone says. Me on Monday: *How are you? You left without saying good-bye last night.* You: *I'm fine.* Me on Tuesday: *I found a couple of properties I'm interested in. Can you call me when you have a chance?* You: *Send an e-mail.* Me on Wednesday: *Are you avoiding me?* You: *No.* Me yesterday: *When can we get together to look at more houses?* You: *I'll get back to you.*" I looked up and raised my brow. "What would you call that? Your longest response to me was five words."

She shrugged one shoulder. "I told you, I've been busy."

"Is this because we slept together?"

Sloan's face turned red.

I'd already suspected the answer since she hadn't made eye contact since I got here, and her flush confirmed it.

"Sloan, it's just sex. You were hot. I was hot. We cooled each other off. You got me off. I got you off. We're adults. It's not a big deal. And, if you're afraid I'm going to have sex with you again, I'm not." I sat down on her couch and relaxed to show her I wasn't going to make a move on her.

She frowned. In confusion or disappointment, I couldn't tell. "You're not?"

I shook my head. "Nope. I mean, don't get me wrong; the sex was … good"—I'd almost said *amazing*—"but I can control myself." I didn't know if I was laying it on thick because I wanted to reassure her that I wasn't going to jump her or if I wanted to see how she'd react. I still couldn't tell what she was thinking.

She didn't say anything.

"But, if you're not busy today, I would like you to set up some appointments, so we can look at homes." I leaned to the side and pulled out the papers I had folded in my back pocket. "These are the ones I found, and I'm sure you have some more."

I held them out to her. She hesitantly stepped forward and took them.

"What time are you off work?" she asked me.

"I don't work today."

"No?"

"Nope. I took it off to spend the day with you."

Her head flew up from where it had been bent over the papers I'd given her.

"I'm kidding. Jeez."

She was like a skittish kitten.

"I work tomorrow, so I have today off." I stood. "Call me later if today works."

"Okay."

"Don't flake on me, or I'll find another agent."

"I won't," she said.

"And one more thing."

"What?"

"Date number three."

Sloan opened her mouth, and before she could protest or come up with some excuse, I held up a hand.

"Us fucking doesn't negate our deal." I raised my brow.

"Unless you think you can't keep your hands off me? I already told you, I'm good, so I see no reason for us not to continue. Besides, if we can look at houses, we can go to dinner."

"I never said I was still going to be your realtor."

"You never said you weren't either. So, the question is, can you?"

"Can I what?"

"Keep your hands off me?"

She scoffed. "*Yes*," she answered, as if I'd insulted her.

I grinned. "Great. Then, I'll pick you up on Sunday. Ted and Mary said they have something for us."

"You tricked me."

"Maybe." I leaned over and gave Bear a pet and a scratch behind the ears, and then I went to the front door. "Call me when you've made the appointments." I opened the door and stepped outside. I grinned. "Don't make me come after you again."

TWENTY

SLOAN

CALEB RAN his hand over the countertop, and my eyes traveled from his muscular biceps to his sexy hands. This was why I'd been avoiding him.

I even thought his hands were sexy.

When he'd shown up at my house this morning, the naughty part of me had wanted him to push me against the wall and kiss me.

Instead, he'd brought me coffee and home information sheets. And he'd made it perfectly clear that he didn't want to sleep with me again. But I supposed I wouldn't care about having sex with someone either if it had only been *good*.

That part had stung a little because it had been more than good for me. Every time I lay down for bed, I'd close my eyes and swear I could still feel him inside me, hitting me high and deep as his pelvis rubbed my clit in just the right way. Except he wasn't actually there, and I'd been left jonesing for his body.

After almost a week, one would think I'd get over it, but the last two nights, I'd busted out my vibrator instead.

So, now, here I stood with the man I wanted to have sex with again but yet didn't want to have sex with. This was why I liked being single and abstained from sex. Things were simply easier that way.

"So, what do you think of this one?" I asked him. I needed to talk and get out of my own head.

"I like it." Caleb pulled out his phone. "I'm adding it to my Maybe list."

His thumb scrolled through and hit some buttons, and I remembered the way it had flicked across my nipples. I didn't remember them being so sensitive before. I moved my gaze away from his hands, but that was a mistake because they landed on his face. He licked his lips as he concentrated, and I remembered the way he'd kissed me. Caleb was one hell of a kisser.

That's it.

"I'm going outside," I announced. "I need to make a phone call. Come out when you're ready. We have a bit before our next appointment." I bolted for the door before he had a chance to answer because, truth be told, I wasn't completely sure that I could keep my hands to myself.

Later that evening, I said good-bye to Caleb and headed over to my parents' for dinner. I was in a foul mood though and had considered canceling. My family didn't deserve my wrath.

Caleb had been a perfect gentleman—as gentlemanly as he could manage—all day. He really *didn't* want to have sex with me again. I should have been ecstatic. I should have been grateful. Instead, I was cranky.

I drove into my parents' driveway and parked my car next to my brother's. I walked into the house and smelled home-cooking and instantly decided I was glad I'd made the decision to come.

"Hey, Mom," I said as I entered the kitchen.

"Hey, Sloan," she said from the sink.

"What are you making?"

"Mashed potatoes. Your father put a roast in the Crock-Pot this morning."

"That explains what smells so delicious. Do you need help with anything?"

"You can cut up the potatoes that I am peeling."

I grabbed a cutting board from the cupboard and a knife from the drawer, and then I started chopping.

"Where are Dad, Trav, and Sydney?" I asked.

"Your father and brother are downstairs. Sydney couldn't make it tonight. I'm not sure what the two guys are doing." My mom finished her peeling and brought the rest of the potatoes over to me.

She pushed my hair over my ear, and I looked up at her. My mom had blonde hair, but her eyes were hazel. Kind of like Caleb's.

Gah!

"What's wrong?" my mom asked. "I feel like I haven't talked to you in a while."

My mom and I were close. I considered her one of my best friends, but sometimes, I felt odd, talking to her about some stuff. Like I would never tell her about vandalizing Neil's car. I knew she wouldn't approve.

"Melanie finally broke up with Neil."

"Good for her." Mom had met him once and didn't like him any more than I did.

"Yeah."

"What made her decide to finally cut him loose?" My mom picked up the potatoes I'd cut and put them in the pot.

"He cheated on her."

My mom looked up and gasped. "He didn't?"

"He did. And he also gave her gonorrhea."

"You're joking."

I shook my head. "I wish I were. She went to the doctor on Monday."

"I never liked that boy."

"You and me both."

All the potatoes were in the pot. My mom filled it up with water and set it on the stove. After she turned the burner on, she faced me. "Is that all that's bothering you?"

I shrugged. I didn't know how much to tell her all about my involvement with Caleb. She probably wouldn't approve of the fake-girlfriend thing.

"I don't know. It's complicated."

"I love complicated."

I laughed. "No, you don't. You are happily married to a man who gives you a nice, normal, boring life."

"Honey, don't worry. You can have that someday soon, too," she joked.

"Promise?"

"I promise. Now, tell me."

"Neil has a brother, and I've been helping him out with something. He's also looking at houses."

My mother frowned. "Are you sure that's a good idea? What if he's like his brother?"

"Oh no, Caleb is nothing like Neil."

My mother raised her brow. Yeah, I noticed how quickly I'd defended him, too.

"Then, what's wrong?"

"I met his boss and his boss's wife. Caleb is like a son to them; they don't have any children of their own, and Caleb has worked for his boss since high school. They got the impression that we were dating, and it made them so happy that neither of us corrected them."

It wasn't exactly true, but if I told my mom Caleb had blackmailed me to play the part, she wouldn't like him.

And I guessed that meant I wanted my mom to like him.

"So, you're feeling guilty about lying?" she asked.

"No." I rethought my answer. "I mean, yes, a little, but that's not the problem."

"Ahh …" she said.

"What? What's 'ahh'?"

"You like him."

"No, I don't."

My mother laughed. "*The lady doth protest too much, methinks.*"

I groaned. "Mom, not Shakespeare."

"Okay. How about, I think you denied that rather quickly?"

I wrinkled my nose at her.

"Does Mel have a problem with you spending time with Caleb?"

"No. None."

"Then, what is it?"

I didn't say anything.

"Honey, not everyone is going to be like the men you've dated in the past. Not every man is going to steal from you or cheat on you or ghost you when he moves out of town."

"I've picked some real winners, huh?"

"That doesn't mean that Caleb will be like them. You just told me that he's not like his brother."

"I know. It's just that I don't want to like him. I don't even know if he likes me."

"Has he kissed you or anything?"

I felt my cheeks heat. He'd done way more than kiss me.

"I'll take that as a yes."

Sometimes, it was a pain in the butt to ask for advice from someone who'd known you since birth.

"It still doesn't mean he likes me. Men kiss women for more reasons than liking them, Mom."

"I know. I wasn't born yesterday. But he must like you on some level."

"I don't know about that. And, even if he did, I don't even know *if* I want to like him."

"That's just your head talking. What does your heart say?"

"I don't know. What if he's the kind of guy who doesn't do serious?" I said, avoiding her answer because I didn't want to think about it too closely.

"Sloan, you haven't had a serious relationship—heck, any relationship—in a long time. You don't have to get married to the first guy you date. You're overthinking. Have fun. Enjoy yourself." She leaned closer to me and grinned. "*Enjoy Caleb*. You deserve it."

I chewed on my lip. I didn't know if I could let myself enjoy anything when it came to him.

My mom put her hand on my arm. "Think about it, honey. You don't have to make a decision today."

She always knew just what to say.

TWENTY-ONE
CALEB

I PICKED up Sloan for dinner on Sunday night, and I could tell right away that something was on her mind.

"You okay?" I asked.

"Yeah."

I knew I'd told her that she had to go through with the five dates, but I really didn't want to force it if she was feeling bad. It was one thing to tease her and irritate her, but it was another to make her do something if she was uncomfortable.

I should have never slept with her.

"Listen, if you're not okay with doing this, I will call Ted right now and tell him you're sick. Or that something came up."

A slow smile crossed her lips, and she visibly relaxed. "No, I'm fine." She looked at me. I thought it was the first time she'd looked me in the eyes since we screwed. "Really, I'm fine. Let's go to dinner."

I studied her for a minute to make sure she was telling the truth. "Okay, but you say the word, and we'll leave. I'll slip you a can of soup to put in the toilet, so you can say you threw up."

Sloan laughed, and the sound made me feel good.

Her avoidance all week and then her reserved demeanor on Friday had made me realize how much I liked having her around and making her smile.

When we got to Ted and Mary's, I made sure not to touch her at all. She obviously didn't want to sleep with me, and I didn't want her to think I was trying to force her or trick her into going to bed with me again. I liked my women willing, thank you very much.

So, when she wrapped her arm around my waist and kissed my neck just as the door opened, I was floored. And turned on. I sported instant wood, remembering those same lips sucking on my cock.

I pushed Sloan in front of me. "Ladies first," I said with a shaky voice.

She gave me a weird look but went in ahead of me while I quickly readjusted my dick in my pants. I stepped up behind her and put a hand on her shoulder, so she would stay in front of me.

"How are you two?" Mary asked.

"Good," Sloan and I both said at the same time.

Everyone chuckled, and tension eased out of my body.

"Come into the family room. Ted's in there, watching the game. Dinner won't be done for ten minutes or so."

Sloan followed Mary, and I followed Sloan, hoping all evidence of my arousal would dissipate by the time we made it to the family room.

"Ted, Caleb and Sloan are here."

Ted spun around in his recliner and smiled when he saw

us. "Hey, guys. Thanks for coming over." He pushed the bottom of his chair down and stood.

"Thanks for having us," Sloan said.

"You know I'm never going to turn down Mary's cooking," I said.

"Doesn't your mother ever feed you, Caleb?" she asked.

I grinned. "Yes, but her cooking isn't as good as yours."

She playfully pushed my arm. "Oh, you."

I looked at Sloan. "She thinks I'm joking, but I'm serious."

Sloan slipped her arm around mine. "I agree, Mary. You are an excellent cook." She leaned forward and whispered, "Don't tell my mom, but you're better than her, too."

Mary blushed at the compliment, and I made a mental note to tell Sloan how good of an actress she was tonight. It seemed like I didn't have to worry about her being uncomfortable.

Ted put his arm around Mary. "I don't think we should wait until after dinner. I think we should do it now."

Mary's eyes lit up. "You think so?"

"What are you two talking about?" I asked.

"I told you that we had something for you," Ted said.

"Go get them, Ted," Mary said, nudging her husband with her hip.

Ted grinned and left the room.

I could tell they were both excited, but I was beginning to feel uncomfortable.

Ted came back with an envelope and handed it to me.

"What is it?" I asked.

"Open it and find out," Mary said.

I slowly opened the envelope and pulled out four tickets to—

"Hawaii," Sloan said breathlessly next to me.

I looked at her and then at Ted and Mary.

He put his arm around his wife again. "We think of you like a son, Caleb, and Mary and I are so happy for you and Sloan. You know that Mary and I have been planning to go to Hawaii, and we want the two of you to come with us."

"Oh my God," Sloan said beside me.

I looked at her, and she looked like she was in shock.

Fuck, fuck, fuck.

I had no idea what to do. This gift was beyond generous, but I couldn't accept it. And I was sure Sloan didn't want to get stuck with me—I looked down at the tickets—for five days. I need to speak with her.

"It's a little less than a month away. We wanted to make sure you could both secure time off," Ted said. "But, Caleb, I have it on good authority that your boss is going to let you take vacation." He winked.

"What about you, Sloan?" Mary asked.

"That's the nice thing about being my own boss. I might have a closing, but I'll have one of my coworkers fill in. I know a few who owe me one." She took a deep breath. "But, listen, this is too much."

Mary waved Sloan's comment away. "Pish posh. We want to do this and are so happy you two are coming with us."

I shook my head. Sloan was right. "You guys, this is too generous," I said. "I—"

A timer buzzed in the kitchen.

"Oh, that's the oven," Mary said.

Another timer dinged.

"And that's the microwave. Ted, come and help me, please. We can give these two some time to talk." She winked, and the two of them left the room.

I walked over to the couch and sank down onto it. I put my head in my hands and moaned.

I felt the cushion next to me sink.

I looked up. "All I wanted to do was show Ted that I had ties to Minnesota and that I wasn't going to bail on the store. I never wanted him to buy us a trip."

"They really love you, Caleb."

"Yeah, well, they shouldn't."

"You're being too hard on yourself. You're a good person. And, while your methods might not always be great, you have good intentions."

I leaned back in my seat and snorted.

Sloan grabbed the tickets out of my hand. "I have to say, this is a great fourth date."

I stared at her.

"What?" she said. "No guy has ever taken me to Hawaii, much less on the fourth date."

"You're not seriously considering going?"

"Why wouldn't I?"

I lowered my voice. "You realize that we're going to have to share a room. Maybe even a bed." I brought my voice up to a normal level. "Besides, I can't take them. I feel like shit, even thinking of saying yes. It's too nice for someone who is lying to them."

Sloan turned to face me and grabbed my shoulders. "Caleb, remember how I told you that telling them would only make *you* feel better? You can't do it."

"So, you're saying we should go?"

She dropped her arms. "Yes. If we say no, their feelings are going to be hurt. Did you see how happy they were to give us these tickets?"

"It was kind of hard not to."

"Exactly. If we tell them we can't go, they're going to be crushed."

She was right.

"Think of it this way. Ted sells you the store, we break up, and then you pay Ted and Mary back, plus interest."

"That's not a bad idea."

Sloan smiled. "I know it's not."

I picked up her hand before I could think too hard about it. "You know, a couple of weeks ago, I would have had to blackmail or bribe you to come with me."

She took her free hand and grabbed my face like I was a kid and shook it back and forth. "Just to be clear, I'm doing this as a favor to you."

"Does this mean, I'm paying for everything?"

"You're damn right you are."

Despite the hit my checkbook was going to take, I grinned at her. There was no one else I would rather take to Hawaii than Sloan.

TWENTY-TWO
SLOAN

CALEB HAD BEEN quiet throughout dinner. I could tell he'd been trying to sound like he was looking forward to the trip, but something had been missing. The good thing was, I didn't think Ted or Mary had noticed.

On the drive home, Caleb didn't say a word. He was so wrapped up in his own thoughts that he almost missed a Stop sign until a car honked at us. By the time he pulled into my driveway, I knew I had to do something, or he was going to make himself crazy.

I reached over and turned off the engine.

He turned his head toward me. "What did you do that for?"

"Come inside," I said. "You need a beer and some Bear snuggles."

He tried to smile. "Thank you, but—"

"I wasn't asking." I pulled the key out of the ignition. "Let's go."

Caleb sighed and followed me into the house where we

were both greeted by Bear. I let him into the backyard to do his business and grabbed two beers from my fridge. I brought them back to the living room where Caleb was already camped out on my couch and handed him one.

"I thought you liked wine?"

I took a long drink. "I do like wine. But I like beer, too. Is that not allowed?"

He laughed. "No. I just didn't realize you drank beer. Some people don't like it."

A bark came from the back door, so I went to let my dog in. "Come on, Bear. Caleb needs some love."

Caleb snorted, but he seemed all too happy when Bear jumped up on the couch and attempted to lie as much of his body on top of him as possible.

I took a sip of my beer and sat down next to Caleb. "Did I mention that Bear thinks he's still the size of a puppy?"

He laughed and scratched the dog behind the ears. "Nope." He leaned toward Bear. "Are you a big baby?"

Bear licked Caleb's cheek.

"I'll take that as a yes."

I picked up my remote and turned on the television. "What do you want to watch? What will distract you?"

He shrugged. "I don't know. I don't watch much TV."

I wrinkled my nose at him.

He laughed. "Don't look at me like that. It's not because I don't like it or think I'm too good to watch TV. I just don't have a lot of time. At least, not lately."

"If you say so."

"It's true."

"So, when you do find time to watch TV, what do you like watching?"

"Sports."

I stuck my finger in my mouth. "Boring."

Caleb laughed again. "Turn on whatever you think is good."

"Hmm." I had to think about this one. The perfect show came to mind. Actually, two of them, but I picked the one I thought Caleb would like the best. "Have you ever watched *Animal Kingdom?*"

He curled his lip. "I'm not big on nature shows."

I laughed. "It's not even close to a nature show."

"Then, what is it?"

"You'll see."

We were about five minutes in when Caleb said, "I totally see why you like this show. A lot of dudes with their shirts off."

I smiled and shrugged. "It doesn't hurt. But keep watching."

When the show ended fifty minutes and another beer later, Caleb said, "Holy shit," in amazement. "That was awesome."

"I know, right?"

He looked at me. "And why did you think I would like this?"

"What's not to like? There's action and sex. Also, lying to your boss pales way, way, way in comparison to these guys."

"You're right about that."

"Do you want to watch the next episode?"

Caleb looked at his phone. "I would, but it's getting late. Tomorrow is Monday."

I switched the TV to some random show and turned the volume down low. I looked over at Bear, who was sleeping in Caleb's lap. "I think you made a friend."

He scratched behind Bear's ears. "That's good. I like him."

"Even if he's sprawled in your lap like he owns it?"

"Yeah." Caleb looked at me, and suddenly, I was aware that he was in my house late at night.

My eyes traced the lines of his face. He really was a handsome man. It wasn't any wonder why I had broken my celibacy with him.

Caleb swallowed. "Right now, I'd rather have——" He shook his head.

"What?" I had to know what he was going to say.

"I can't say. You'll probably kick me out."

Now, I was dying to know the rest of his sentence. "I promise not to kick you out."

"I was going to say, I'd rather have Bear's owner sit on my lap like she owns it."

Bear lifted his head at the sound of his name. He yawned and jumped off the couch.

I moved closer. "But I thought you said the sex was simply *good*. Why would you want me in your lap? Is this because you can't date anyone else while we're 'dating'?" I asked, using air quotes.

Caleb laughed and pulled me onto his lap. "I lied." He ran his nose along my jaw and down my neck. "Being inside you was fucking phenomenal."

I shivered.

"I only said it was good, so I wouldn't scare you away. Because I was worried, if I told you that I touched myself every night while I thought of you, you'd probably sprint away."

Caleb looked up at me. His big hazel eyes were full of heat, and I did the only thing a red-blooded heterosexual woman could do.

I kissed him.

I quickly moved, so I was straddling him. I wanted to feel his thickness between my legs.

Caleb squeezed the top of my thighs and moaned.

I loved how turned on he was because of me. It made me feel powerful.

We made out for a few minutes, kissing each other on every inch of bare skin within reach of our mouths, and he thumbed my nipples through my shirt and bra while I rotated my hips over him.

"Fuck, baby. You're going to make me come in my pants like a teen."

I kissed him again and slid off his lap and onto the floor between his legs.

"God, you look so sexy right now," he said. "It makes me wish you would …"

I tugged my bottom lip between my teeth. "Makes you wish what?" I ran the palm of my hand over his bulging erection and unbuttoned his jeans. "That I would go down on you? Suck you off? Make you come?"

He put his hand on mine. "You have to stop teasing me."

I pushed his hand away. "Who said I'm teasing?"

I lowered the zipper and reached for the waist of his pants. He lifted his hips, and I pulled his jeans down.

"There he is," I said breathlessly and grabbed on to Caleb's shaft.

I knew I would sound weird, saying it out loud, but he had a beautiful dick. It was long and thick and the same girth from the base to almost the tip, where his mushroom head was bulbous, just like I liked penises to be.

A drop of pre-cum leaked out, so I swiped my thumb over it and spread it around his crown.

Caleb groaned.

I lowered my mouth to him and took a deep pull. I moaned at his flavor. He tasted as good as he looked. I'd already known this from last weekend, but it was nice to know it hadn't been my imagination.

Caleb grabbed on to my hair. "*Fuck-fuck-fuck-fuck-fuck-fuck.* Did you take lessons in giving head or something?"

He made a gagging sound as I sucked him into the back of my throat. He pulled on my hair, hard enough that I knew he wanted me to let go and look up.

"What's wrong?" I asked.

"This isn't fair. You blew me first last time."

I smiled. This was why I liked him. He might say stupid shit sometimes and tease me, but when it came down to it, he was a gentleman. Kind of. I was pretty sure whoever had coined the term was not referring to men eating women out.

"Don't fret," I said, enveloping his cock with my hand. "I like giving head." In fact, I loved it. "Haven't you ever met a girl who does before?"

"Yes. I just …"

"What?"

"Never expected it from you."

I lifted my eyebrows. "That's what makes it that much more fun." I looked down at him from my nose. "Now, be quiet. I have a dick to suck."

"I think I've died and gone to heaven."

TWENTY-THREE
CALEB

A WEEK AND A HALF LATER, Ted stopped me at work. "Caleb, how about you and I grab a beer after work?"

"Sure. I'll text Sloan to tell her that I might be a little late."

He clapped me on the back. "Sounds good," he said and headed back to his office.

I pulled out my phone to shoot Sloan a quick message. I hadn't been making it up when I told Ted I needed to let her know.

Since the night we'd received the trip to Hawaii, I had felt less guilty because, at this point, it felt like Sloan and I were really dating.

If you considered fucking like bunnies and binge-watching *Animal Kingdom* dating. The fact that neither of our families knew about our situation was probably an argument against it being dating. But the two of us were enjoying ourselves, so I ignored that part of my brain.

A couple of hours later, the two of us were ready to go.

"Do you mind if I drive?" Ted asked.

It was an odd question because we usually drove separately. Then, we could go home after, and no one would have to give the other person a ride.

"It's not far," Ted said when I didn't answer.

"Okay. Sure."

We got in Ted's SUV.

"Where are we going?"

The two of us had only about three places that we frequented.

"Someplace new. You'll see."

My suspicions rose even more. If I didn't know Ted so well, I would worry he was going to murder me or something.

The good thing was that he was right. The place we were going was only about ten minutes away. But it wasn't a bar or a restaurant.

It was Ted's jewelry store.

Ted had asked me to help him pick out gifts for Mary in the past, but he had never kept it a secret or tricked me into coming.

"Why are we here?"

Ted turned off the engine and exited the vehicle. I had no choice but to follow or sit in the car and wonder what I was missing.

There were several people in the store, but the minute an older gentleman in an expensive suit saw Ted, he said, "Excuse me," to the couple he'd been speaking with. "Henry, can you help this couple, please?"

A younger man stepped in as the older man came over to us.

"Ted," he said, holding out his hand. "It's good to see you."

"You're just saying that because, every time I come in, I spend money," Ted said.

The man turned to me and held out his hand. "Hello again, Caleb."

"Hello, Frank."

Frank, who was Ted's jewelry guy, looked at me and said, "Are you ready to get started?"

I looked at Ted. "Uh ... sure?"

Ted chuckled. "I didn't tell Caleb why we were coming today."

"Ah," Frank said. "This will be exciting then." He waved his hand to the corner of the store. "I set some stuff out for you."

Still having no clue as to what these two were talking about, I blindly followed Frank and Ted.

Frank opened a cabinet with a key. "I set these aside for you earlier today. Ted told me what you were looking for, but I still have a couple of other options for you." He set a velvet box on the counter.

In the box were several rings, all with diamonds and birthstones on each side.

Just when I was beginning to feel less guilty, Ted had to do something else to bring it all back. Which made me sound like an asshole for complaining.

By the time these five dates were over, I wasn't even going to want to buy the store anymore.

Ted clapped me on the shoulder. "Go ahead, Caleb.

Look. I told Frank what Sloan had said up at the lake, but you know her best."

I laughed inside at the joke. I didn't know her that well.

Just tell Ted you're not ready.

Excellent plan, brain.

"Mary thought Hawaii would be the perfect place to propose. It's not often you get to travel to a beautiful location to ask the woman you love to marry you."

"Oh, she did, huh?"

Fucking Mary.

Now, my excuse sounded like a bunch of horseshit.

Also, I secretly sent out an apology to Mary for swearing about her, but seriously, Ted and Mary were making my life very difficult.

I tentatively picked up a ring. It was what Sloan had said she wanted, but the band was too thick. "I need a thinner band." I set it down and picked up another. "Something like this." I looked at the stones though and saw that it was a round cut. Sloan had said she wanted princess.

Sometimes, us guys could pay attention.

I set the ring down and went for another. It was a princess cut with two smaller gemstones in round cut. The two cuts looked good together. And the band was a thin white metal. I couldn't tell white gold from platinum.

I held it up. "This one."

Frank looked down. "Are you sure? You don't want one of these other ones with a little more sparkle?" He pointed to one ring that had small diamonds running down each side of the band. Another had a band that twisted with tiny diamonds.

I shook my head. "They're pretty, but no. Sloan said she wanted simple."

"All right. This one it is," Frank said and grabbed the ring from me. He took out a pad of paper and wrote on it. "We'll take out the two emeralds on the sides. What birthstones do you want in there?"

I shrugged. "I don't know what they're called, but our birthdays are February and October. All I know is, she said pink and purple."

Frank wrote that down, too.

A thought occurred to me. "Will these even be done before we leave for our trip?" I tried not to sound too excited when I asked the question.

Frank winked. "Don't you worry about that. Ted has been my customer for over thirty years." He leaned in closer and whispered, "I'm moving you to the front of the line."

"Thank you," I said in a tight voice. "That's so kind of you."

"Only the best for Ted. And Ted's friends, of course."

I put a down payment on the ring and left a few hundred dollars lighter and with an empty pit in my stomach.

I sent Sloan a text, telling her I wasn't going to make it tonight.

I had no idea how I was going to tell Sloan that I'd bought an engagement ring and that Ted and Mary wanted me to propose to her on the trip. She was going to flip.

TWENTY-FOUR

SLOAN

"HEY, SLOAN. COME UP HERE?"

"One second."

Caleb and I were looking at a house that had just come on the market, and he had already gone upstairs while I was still looking around on the main level. We had plans to go to dinner, and he'd said he had to talk to me about what had happened with Ted yesterday, but I had wanted to show him the house first.

I took my time, walking up the stairs to look for any major flaws and thankfully found none.

"Where are you?" I asked.

"In the big bedroom."

The top floor had three bedrooms with another on the lower level. It was in a nice neighborhood, and the price was decent.

"Look at this view," Caleb said as I walked into the bedroom.

The back of the house had no neighbors. It sat up

against a grove of trees, and the view and privacy bumped up the price from decent to great.

Even better, the primary bedroom had two French doors that went outside to a small terrace. Caleb opened the doors, and we stepped outside. Even though there were neighboring houses on either side, unless the neighbors were standing in the backyard, no one could see where we stood.

I went up to the rail and looked down. "This would be perfect to sit out here and drink coffee." I closed my eyes and imagined it.

Caleb came up behind me and wrapped one arm around my waist. "I can think of one other thing to do up here."

I turned my head and rubbed his cheek with the side of my face. "Oh, yeah? What's that?"

"Hmm … something like this."

His other hand slid up my leg and under my dress. I closed my eyes and soaked up his touch. His fingers brushed my clit, and I suddenly couldn't wait to get home. I figured Caleb was teasing me, letting me know what was to come later, so I was completely surprised when he pulled my underwear aside and slid his fingers through my wetness.

"Oh, yeah." He kissed my neck. "I love how you're always ready for me."

"I'm not always ready."

He chuckled. "Coulda fooled me." He pushed a finger inside me.

I moaned. I should tell him to stop. I was technically working after all. But I hadn't seen him for two days, and my body already missed him.

His hand went straight for my magical spot. At this

point, he knew exactly how to tease me and exactly how to make me come.

Another digit joined the first, and I rolled my hips on his hand. "Oh. Yes. Right there."

"Right here?" he asked, putting a little extra pressure on my G-spot.

I softly cried out. "Yes. Please. Don't stop."

I threw my arm around the back of his neck and used his body to ride his hand. I was thankful for the secluded spot because I was right there. I felt my inner muscles tighten, but a split second before I exploded, Caleb pulled his hand away.

I cried out again, this time in frustration, and let my knees buckle. "I hate you."

Caleb held me up and chuckled. "Don't worry, baby. I got you."

"Lies."

He laughed again and took my arm from around his neck and placed it on the railing. He nudged me forward. "Lean over."

I rested my elbows on the banister as Caleb slipped my underwear off.

"What are you doing?"

"I told you, I got you." He flipped the back of my dress up. "So pretty. Pink and wet."

I heard and felt him bend down. I had no clue as to what he planned to do, so when his mouth touched my clit, I jolted.

I lifted the front of my dress and met Caleb's eyes. He smiled and sucked me into his mouth. I tried to look away, but the eye contact he was giving me was hot as hell.

He slightly drew away. "I wish you could taste you like I can," he said before putting his mouth back between my legs.

My legs started shaking, and my orgasm was building up again. "Are you going to let me come this time?"

Caleb smiled but didn't answer.

I closed my eyes and put my forehead down on my arms. It was getting harder for me to stand up.

I began to rock my hips again when Caleb pulled away. I thought he merely needed a break, but when I felt the cool air travel over my pussy, I knew he was gone.

I lifted my head and looked over my shoulder just in time to watch Caleb's face as he thrust his cock inside me.

I gripped the rail. "Oh shit."

"*Yes*," Caleb hissed. "Someday, I'm going to take you bare."

I pushed my hips back at him to let him know I liked the idea. Not only was he a fantastic lover, but he was also always safe, to the point that I was almost convinced that he had a magical pocket in his pants that had a portal to condoms.

He grabbed my hips and thrust into me slow but deep. He gradually picked up his pace, and I knew it wouldn't be long for me. He'd already prepped my G-spot with his fingers, so every time his shaft hit, I was that much closer.

When I didn't think I could stand the torture of hanging on the precipice any longer, Caleb slipped his hand around to my front and pinched my clit between his fingers.

I screamed as my orgasm flooded my body.

Caleb quickly slapped a hand over my mouth, and I held on to his arm as my body shook.

Caleb grunted. "You're so tight; it's hard to stay inside you."

I pulled on his hand to let him know I wouldn't scream anymore, and he slid it down to my neck as his other hand dug into my hips before he started thrusting again.

Normally, I didn't like anything tight around my throat, but the way Caleb clutched me, my body against his as he stroked into me over and over, was incredibly sensual. It was like he couldn't get enough of me, yet at the same time, he was so into what he was doing that he didn't even notice how tightly he was holding me.

I had just orgasmed, yet I could feel that telltale tingle deep inside me again.

Caleb's mouth was by my ear. "You're getting tight on me again, baby. Are you going to come?"

"I don't know. I've never come twice in a row before." Like men, I needed a recovery period.

The hand on my hip drifted down my lower abdomen until he was cupping my pussy. He pushed the heel of his hand down right over my pubic bone the same time he thrust into me.

"Oh my God."

"Do you want me to stop?" he teased.

"Don't you fucking dare." I put a hand over his lower one. "Again."

Caleb sucked on my neck as he rode me hard from behind. I knew he was close. I was okay with not coming again, but as he slammed into me one last time, he bit down on my neck, and I exploded once again.

The next thing I was aware of was that the two of us were sitting on a chair positioned in the corner of the balcony. I was on Caleb's lap, and he was still inside me. We were both breathing hard and not moving.

"Holy crap, baby, that was—"

We heard the sound of the front door opening, and voices carried upstairs.

"Shit." I quickly stood, pulling Caleb from my body.

He hissed, but he quickly got up and went to the bathroom. The toilet flushed, and he came out two seconds later.

"I can't find my underwear," I said in a panic. I had smoothed my dress down, and it almost went to my knees, but I would be mortified if the homeowners or other buyers found my panties lying somewhere.

Caleb patted his shorts. "They're in my pocket."

"Whew." I flattened my hair down. "Do I look okay?"

"You look like you've been fucked."

"Caleb."

He laughed. "You look fine, except …" He stepped forward and pulled one side of my hair to the front of my shoulder. "I left a little love bite on you."

I put my hand to my neck. "Thanks. I think we should get out of here."

"That sounds like a great idea."

Footsteps sounded on the steps as voices got louder, and soon, three people came into view. I recognized the other realtor, but I didn't know her well. She had two women with her.

"Hello," she said.

"Hi." I put my hand on Caleb's arm "Let's go, shall we? Let them take a look."

"Right," he said.

The trio walked into the bedroom.

We were right at the bedroom door when Caleb stopped and turned around. "Check out the balcony. It has an awesome view."

I narrowed my eyes at him and walked out the door.

Caleb laughed and followed me.

"You're a turd," I whispered.

As soon as we were downstairs, he said, "Would you take back the turd comment if I told you I wanted to buy the house?"

In all my excitement of putting a deal through for Caleb, I completely forgot to ask what had happened with Ted, and Caleb never brought it up.

TWENTY-FIVE
CALEB

THE SOUND of a phone ringing woke me from my sleep, and Sloan shifted in my arms.

"Turn it off," she mumbled.

"That's your phone, babe." I didn't even know where mine was. I should probably find it first thing when I got up.

"Ignore it then," she said into her pillow.

I lifted my head and looked at the clock. "Babe, it's almost four in the morning on a Saturday. It's probably important."

Sloan smacked her hand down on her nightstand to search for her phone. She held it up, and I could see that it was Melanie calling, even before Sloan said it out loud.

"What the hell? It's the middle of the night."

"It's probably important."

Sloan swiped the screen and put the cell to her ear. "Hello?"

"Hey, sorry to call so late, but is Caleb there?" Melanie asked.

159

I could hear everything since Sloan and I were close together.

"Um, yes. Hold on." Sloan looked over her shoulder at me and held out her phone. "It's for you."

She looked confused and curious, so I shrugged to let her know that I was as clueless as she was.

"Hey. It's Caleb."

"I'm sorry to ask you this, but could you come to my house and get your brother?"

"What?" I pulled my arm out from under Sloan's head and sat up.

"Yeah. He showed up here, drunk, and won't leave. I'd let him stay, but I'm worried that will send the wrong message."

"No, no. Don't apologize. I'll be there as soon as I can."

I heard Melanie sigh with relief. "Thank you."

I hung up Sloan's phone and was ready to hand it to her when I realized she wasn't in the room.

I quickly pulled on my clothes from the day before and went in search of her.

"Hey, can you let Bear in from outside while I get dressed?" she asked when I found her by the back door.

I kissed her. "Yeah. Here's your phone."

Sloan ran off to her bedroom, and since Bear was still sniffing around for the perfect place to go to the bathroom, I did a quick search of the kitchen and living room.

My phone was halfway between two couch cushions, and I saw that I had several missed calls. The first one was over a half hour ago, and I cursed myself for not having my phone near me earlier.

Bear pawed at the door the same time Sloan emerged from her room, dressed and ready to go.

When we got to Melanie's house, Sloan opened the door before I even shut off my car.

"He's in here," Melanie said after Sloan and I exited my vehicle.

As I walked past Melanie, I heard Sloan ask, "Are you okay?"

"Yeah," Melanie said in a less than convincing tone.

I found Neil rummaging around in the kitchen.

"Hey," I said cautiously.

My brother didn't get drunk a lot. He drank with clients and at my parents', but he usually stopped well before being drunk. I also hadn't talked to him since I punched him in the face. He had avoided going to Mom and Dad's the last time they asked us over for dinner. I'd assumed it was because his face hadn't healed yet.

He looked over at the sound of my voice and grinned. "Hey, Caleb."

Okay, so he wasn't holding a grudge against me for hitting him. Or he was too intoxicated to care.

"Hey. What are you doing?"

"Looking for food. Melanie always keeps my favorite snacks at her house, but I can't find any of them," he whined.

"Neil, you and Melanie aren't dating anymore."

My brother opened another cupboard, ignoring me.

"*Neil.*"

He didn't even bother to look at me.

I had been hoping I wouldn't have to get physical, so I'd been keeping my distance, but that wasn't going to work. I stepped closer, grabbed my brother's shoulders, and turned him around to face me.

"Neil, she doesn't have any of your food because the two of you broke up. Remember?"

Neil looked confused, and then, as realization kicked in, he went from puzzled to sad. "I fucked up."

"Yeah, ya did, buddy. You weren't the best boyfriend. Why can't you keep it in your pants?"

He shook his head. "I don't know."

"Maybe you need to figure that out. Talk to someone about your habitual cheating. Have you ever been faithful to a girlfriend?"

Neil's brow furrowed as he looked off into the distance. We didn't have time for his drunk brain to go through every woman he'd dated since high school.

"You know what? Never mind."

Neil turned his eyes back to me. "I love her."

Ah, shit. Please don't let him start crying.

"I know you do, but you done fucked up. How would you feel if you found out Melanie had cheated on you?"

His eyes blazed. "I would be furious."

"And hurt?"

"Yes."

"So, how do you think Melanie felt when she found out about you cheating?"

"Oh. I never thought of it like that."

Seriously? The guy was thirty years old and never thought

about how the woman in the relationship felt. *How did we come from the same parents?*

"I take back my *maybe* comment. You need to talk to someone. Like yesterday."

Neil nodded. "Yeah. Maybe I'll do that."

I shook my head. "No maybe." I started nodding. "You're going to do that. Say it with me. *I'm going to talk to someone.*"

"I'm going to talk to someone," Neil parroted.

"Good. Now, let's go, so Melanie can go back to bed."

My brother sighed in defeat.

I put my arm around him and led him out of the kitchen. "How did you get here? Please tell me you didn't drive."

He shook his head. "Uber."

Thank God for that.

Sloan and Melanie were standing close together in the living room.

"Neil, I need you to tell Melanie that you're sorry for coming here and scaring her."

My brother looked sheepish. "I'm sorry for showing up like I did." He stepped forward. "But I—"

I yanked him back by his collar. "No buts. Just apologize."

"I'm sorry."

I looked at Sloan. "Is it okay if we drop him off before going back to your place?" I glanced at Melanie. "Or did you want to stay here?"

Melanie pushed Sloan away from her. "You go. I'll be fine."

Sloan hesitated. "Are you sure? I can totally stay."

"No. I'm fine." Melanie looked at Neil, who was now practically falling asleep on my shoulder. "He didn't hurt me or anything. I just couldn't get him to leave."

"If you're sure?"

Melanie smiled. "Yes. Go. I just want to go back to bed and sleep."

"Okay." She turned to Neil and me. "Let's get this jackass home," she said.

I chuckled.

Neil lifted his head. "Jackass? Where?"

I patted him on the chest. "In the mirror, buddy."

"Ha. Good one," Neil said.

It was time to get this jackass home.

TWENTY-SIX
SLOAN

I GROANED in pleasure as the massage chair kneaded my muscles, and the woman at my feet took care of my toes.

"Feel good?" Melanie asked.

"Yes. Feels great. I needed a pedicure quite badly. You?"

She grinned. "It feels wonderful. And, yeah, you can't go to Hawaii with ugly toes."

I chuckled. "The horror," I joked.

"Are you ready for your trip?" she asked.

"Yeah. I'm pretty much packed." I looked at Mel. "I wish you could go with me. When was the last time we took a trip together?"

"Hmm." She laughed. "I can't even remember."

"Me either. That's bad. And this is why you should go to Hawaii with me."

"Nah. I don't want to hear all the sex you and Caleb will be having from the room next to yours."

"You can get a room a few doors down from us."

Melanie barked out a laugh. "You didn't even deny it."

I shrugged. Caleb was fantastic in bed. There was nothing to deny.

"I would love to go, but this is going to be your romantic getaway."

"Whoa, whoa, whoa. Caleb and I aren't really a couple. We're …" I had to stop and think about this one. "We're partners with benefits. He scratches my back, and I scratch his."

Mel's brow furrowed. "I get why you're helping him, but what is he doing for you?"

Abort. Abort. My brain panicked.

She still didn't know that Caleb had figured out that we had vandalized Neil's car. Or that he had threatened to tell if I didn't agree to his deal. And, now that I liked Caleb, I really didn't want her to know and think badly of him.

"Uh … he's buying a house from me," I said.

She looked skeptical. "Yeah, but that's your job. And he was going to buy a house anyway. From you or someone else. I don't really think it's a fair trade."

"It is, okay?" I blurted out.

"Okay." She shook her head. "You're acting weird."

"I'm just nervous about the trip." It wasn't a total lie. I was excited, but I was anxious, too, about Ted and Mary being there.

"Is that why you wanted me to come with?" She stuck out her lip in mock sadness. "Is someone afraid she likes someone else more than she should?"

"No," I denied.

She snorted. "Yeah, right. Caleb is a great guy. Look how he came to the rescue last weekend when Neil showed up at my house. He didn't even hesitate." She wiggled her eyebrows at me. "If you weren't sleeping with him, I would."

"You can't get involved with your ex's brother."

Melanie shrugged. "Says who? Is there a law I don't know about?"

"Well … no. But you just can't."

"I don't know. Maybe, when you and Caleb 'break up,'" she said, using air quotes, "I can ask him out."

I didn't know what to say. I was getting mad at my friend, and I didn't want to. Caleb wasn't really my boyfriend. I shouldn't be getting upset.

"You know she's messing with you, right?" said the lady giving Melanie a pedicure.

My eyes flew to Melanie's, who was trying not to laugh.

"Why?" I asked.

"Because I want you to realize how much you like him. Duh."

I scowled at her. "I don't like *you* right now."

"You love me. You just don't like the fact that I'm right." She put her hand on my arm. "You might have gotten involved with him for odd reasons, but it doesn't change how you feel." She removed her arm and sat back in her seat.

"How do I know if he likes me?"

She burst out laughing as if I'd told her a great joke. "You're kidding, right?"

I scoffed. "No."

"Trust me. He likes you."

"What are you, psychic?"

"No, I just have two eyes and can see the way he looks at you."

I tried not to smile but didn't really succeed.

Two days later, we were flying into Honolulu. Now that Caleb, Mary, Ted, and I were finally here, I was really excited.

August probably seemed like an odd month to go to Hawaii, but I wasn't complaining since the tickets were free. I had looked up the weather before leaving, and the average wasn't that much higher than back home in Minneapolis, but the humidity was lower.

Some people thought it was cold all the time in Minnesota since we were one of the coldest states in the continental US, but it got hot there, too. And an average humidity of ninety percent was what we had to deal with in the summer.

Hawaii was going to feel great. Especially all those days at the beach or in the ocean. I might burn, but I still loved sitting at the beach.

We picked up our rental car and headed to our hotel. As Caleb and I unpacked some of our stuff in our hotel room, I realized it was a good thing I had taken my mom's advice and not shut Caleb out. It would have been a long and awkward trip.

Instead, it was going to be fun, and as a bonus, I would get to have sex with Caleb every night.

"What are you grinning about over there?" he said from our king-size bed.

I looked over my shoulder. "We're in Hawaii. How can you not be grinning?"

He shook his head and tried to look sad. "And here I

thought, you were happy because you got to be with me for five straight days."

I didn't want to let him know how right he was.

I snorted. "You wish." I put the last of my clothes in a drawer to make it easier to keep them arranged, and then I turned around. "If anything, you should be happy that you get to spend five straight days with *me*."

"Who says I'm not?"

"I don't see a smile on your face," I pointed out.

"Maybe you need to come closer."

I sashayed closer to the bed. When my knees hit the mattress, I said, "I'm closer, and I still don't see a smile."

Caleb grabbed my hand and yanked me down on the bed.

I laughed and rolled over on my back to see Caleb grinning.

"Now, I'm happy," he said and kissed me.

TWENTY-SEVEN
CALEB

"WHEN ARE you going to pop the question?" Ted asked me at breakfast on our third day in Hawaii after Sloan and Mary went to use the restroom. He rolled his eyes. "Mary keeps asking me about it."

"I don't know," I answered honestly because I really didn't know. I was hoping never.

I still hadn't told Sloan about the ring. I had meant to talk to her, but after the amazing sex we'd had, I hadn't wanted to ruin the rest of the evening.

And, up until we'd left, I had secretly hoped Frank wouldn't come through and get the ring finished, but he called me the day before we left. I considered pretending like I hadn't gotten the voice mail, but Ted came out of his office minutes later with a smile on his face. Frank had called Ted, too, when I hadn't answered my phone.

I'd then considered "accidentally" leaving the ring home, but after everything Ted and Mary had done, I'd felt bad, so I'd thrown it in my suitcase right before we left for the airport.

"You'd better get on that. You don't have much time."

"I know. Maybe I just want it to be perfect." *And for the woman I ask to not freak out.*

"You've gone horseback riding, to a luau, sat on the beach. What more could you ask for?"

"I know," I said lamely.

Ted snapped his fingers. "I know what's wrong."

"You do?"

"You're afraid she's going to say no."

I chuckled. *Something like that.* "Maybe."

Ted shook his head. "I don't think you have anything to worry about. I've seen the way she looks at you."

"Really. How's that?" I asked, intrigued now.

"The same way you look at her."

I looked away as my cheeks heated. It was true that I was becoming more and more infatuated with Sloan, the longer we spent time together. I figured it was just because of all the good sex. We'd certainly never discussed feelings with each other. I'd had no idea I was looking at her in a certain way.

"Where's the ring?" Ted asked.

I turned back to him. "In my suitcase."

"Go and get it."

My eyes widened. "What? Now?"

We were in the hotel's restaurant. It would only take me minutes to get to my room and back, but now hardly seemed like the time.

"Yes. You're never going to do it unless someone gives you a good kick in the butt."

"I-I—"

"Just go and get the damn ring, Caleb."

171

I could see this was not an argument I was going to win, so I got up and headed to my room, pulling out my phone as I went.

> Me: Don't freak out.

> Sloan: Starting a text like that only means that I'm probably going to freak out.

> Me: You haven't so far.

> Sloan: Just tell me what's wrong.

> Me: I don't want to.

> Sloan: LOL. Spill it.

> Me: Okay. Brace yourself.

> Sloan: I'm braced.

> Me: I'm going up to my room to grab an engagement ring that Ted helped me buy.

> Me: And then I'm going to come back down to breakfast and propose.

I waited for Sloan to reply, but nothing came up. I unlocked our hotel room and went to my suitcase. The ring was still in the exact pocket where I'd packed it.

I looked at my phone again. Nothing.

> Me: I'm sorry I didn't tell you sooner. I've been trying to find a way to get out of it. I know this is not what you signed up for, but Ted and Mary thought Hawaii would be the perfect place to propose. It didn't seem plausible to say no. I mean, it is Hawaii.

I left the hotel room, staring at my phone. The closer I got to the restaurant, the more I began to panic. I had no idea what she was thinking.

> Me: You can tell me no. My ego will take a hit because, I mean, who wouldn't want to marry this?

I hoped a joke would lighten the seriousness of the situation.

> Me: But you don't have to say yes.

Finally, I could see that Sloan was typing something.

> Sloan: Go ahead and ask. I'll say yes.

No way. I couldn't believe she was going to go along with it.

> Me: Really?

> Sloan: Yes. It's just an engagement. It's not like we're actually getting married.

Me: If I haven't told you yet how amazing you are, I'm telling you now.

Sloan: You told me last night in bed.

Me: But that's when I was inside you. That was sexually motivated. I didn't want you to kick me out.

Sloan: Kick you out of my vagina?

Me: Yeah, I really like it there.

Sloan: I've noticed.

Me: You like me there, too. Anyway, this time, it's coming purely from the heart. You. Are. Amazing.

Sloan: Thank you. Now, hurry up before I change my mind.

I walked back into the restaurant, feeling more confident than I had fifteen minutes ago. I considered sitting down next to her and dragging out the proposal, maybe even getting out of it altogether even though she had given me the go-ahead.

But, when I saw Sloan throw her head back and laugh at something either Mary or Ted had said, a part of me—a part way deep, deep down inside—wanted to see her laugh like that for as long as I could. I wanted to be the one who made her laugh like that.

And, when she looked forward again and her eyes made

contact with mine, she smiled. It was a smile I was coming to love.

I didn't realize I had paused on my way to the table until that moment. I'd been so caught up in watching her.

With a new sense of determination, I zeroed in on Sloan and made my way to the table. When I reached her, I pulled out the ring from my pocket and got down on one knee.

"Sloan Zehler will you marry me?"

TWENTY-EIGHT
SLOAN

CALEB HAD WARNED me that he was going to propose, but he hadn't warned me that the engagement ring was exactly what I wanted. And he hadn't said that the look on his face would look like he was really asking.

My hands flew to my mouth, and tears threatened to spill down my face.

I'm not supposed to be crying. This wasn't a real proposal.

Except I realized that a part of me wanted it to be.

When the hell did I start liking this guy so much? Maybe I should say no.

I wish I could know what Caleb was thinking. *Is he panicking inside or just secretly rolling his eyes?* I had no way of knowing.

But, when I met his eyes, the look there was one I had never seen before. It was the way my dad looked at my mom. It was the way Ted looked at Mary.

So, when I opened my mouth and said, "Yes," I discovered I'd actually meant it.

But, before my own panic could set in, Caleb slipped the ring on my finger and kissed me. Not a peck, but a full-blown kiss, and the crowd went wild. They clapped and whistled, which was good, because I'd almost forgotten the two of us weren't alone.

Caleb slipped into the booth next to me and put his arm around my shoulders as I looked down at the ring. It was perfect.

"I like looking at you with my ring on your finger," he whispered in my ear.

I liked it, too. Maybe too much, but we were in paradise right now. I could let myself enjoy it.

I kissed him on the jaw. "Thank you. It's beautiful."

"I think you should get married here," Mary said.

Caleb and I both looked at the couple across the booth from us. It'd almost slipped my mind they were there.

"Excuse me?" I said.

"I think you should elope. It's so romantic to get engaged in such a beautiful place. Why not get married now?"

"Uh …" Caleb said.

"We don't have a marriage license."

Mary held up her phone. "You can go online and fill it out. You don't have to wait to get married in Hawaii either. You can get married the same day."

Caleb visibly swallowed.

"But I can't get married without my family," I said.

"You can have a party when you get back," Ted offered.

"How about we think about it?" Caleb said.

That's a great idea.

"Yes, let us talk about it," I agreed.

I pulled my phone from the table.

> Me: Getting married would be totally crazy, right?

> Caleb: Yes, totally crazy.

I looked up into his face. Maybe it was just me who was crazy because, for some reason, I didn't believe either of us really felt that way.

After breakfast, Caleb and I went snorkeling. It was pretty hard to talk about weddings when both our heads were underwater. And, thankfully, the beautiful blue of the water and incredible animals swimming by us caused us both to forget all about the marriage talk.

"What's your favorite thing we've done here so far?" I asked him as we drove back to our hotel.

"I don't know. I really liked today."

"Me, too. The water was beautiful. But I really liked the horseback riding. The scenery was gorgeous." I sighed and stared out the window. "I can see why people live here."

"Maybe we should move here," he joked.

"I could get my Hawaii real estate license, but you might have a hard time moving the store." I rubbed my thumb against my fingers. "I imagine it would cost a pretty penny."

Caleb lost his smile. "Yeah, if he even sells it to me."

I sat up. "Has he said more about Rick buying it?"

In the beginning, Caleb had only seemed mad about the prospect of losing the store to Rick, but now that I knew him better, I knew he was also hurt. Rick might be Ted's nephew, but Caleb was much closer to Ted.

"No," Caleb answered.

"That's good, right?"

He shrugged. "I guess."

I wrapped my arm around his and laid my head on his bicep. "Don't lose hope. After all, you're the one he brought to Hawaii."

"Maybe it's just a consolation prize."

I looked up at him. I wanted to turn his face, so I could meet his eyes, but he was driving. "Hey."

"Yeah?"

"Don't give up yet. Okay?"

He glanced at me. "Okay." He turned back to the road and smiled. "And, no matter what happens, I got to spend the best vacation with you."

I laid my head back down and grinned. I felt the same way.

"What are our plans for the rest of the afternoon?" I asked.

"How about make love and then lie on the beach? In the shade," he added, knowing my tendency to burn easily. "And then we're having dinner at that restaurant Mary and Ted suggested."

"That sounds like a plan," I said with a grin.

Caleb had never called having sex lovemaking before.

I tilted my head up. "But I think we should shower first."

The ocean was beautiful, but salt water was drying on the skin.

He smiled down at me. "How about we shower together? And then, after, I'll rub lotion all over your body."

"Ooh. Even better. How about a shower together and then a couples massage?"

Caleb groaned. "You got yourself a deal."

TWENTY-NINE

CALEB

AFTER OUR COUPLES MASSAGE, Sloan and I napped in each other's arms for a little too long. By the time we woke up, I was starving, and the sun was already starting to set.

I knocked on the bathroom door. "You almost ready?" I asked.

The door swung open, and Sloan stood on the other side with an impatient look on her face.

"Damn. You look good enough to eat," I said as I scanned her body.

Her red hair was down around her shoulders, and she was wearing a white dress that was perfect for a casual dinner on the beach.

"But that could be my stomach talking," I told her when I reached her eyes.

She rolled her eyes but couldn't stop the smile that broke out across her face. Gotta love a woman who laughed at your jokes even when she thought they were lame.

"I have my lipstick left, and then I'm done."

I sighed. "Who cares? It's going to come off when you eat, and if for some reason it's still there, it's going to come off when I kiss you later."

She raised her eyebrows and slowly unscrewed her lipstick just to torture me. "Anyone ever tell you that you're crabby when you're hungry?"

"Duh," I said, not bothering to deny it. "You already know this about me. Remember the night you denied me food for hours and hours?"

Sloan smiled as she put on her lipstick. "It was an hour, an hour and a half tops. And I had to work." She looked at me. "You lived, didn't you?"

"Yeah, but not happily."

She set her lipstick down. "I'm ready now," she said, stepping out of the bathroom. "Let's get you fed, grumpy."

I leaned back and patted my stomach. "I am going to miss the fresh seafood something fierce when we go back home."

Sloan picked up her glass. "I agree. It's so much better when it's fresh." She took a long drink and finished off her wine. She looked into the glass as if there might be more hiding. "I'm not ready for the night to end," she said when she looked up at me.

"So, let's go do something. After our nap this afternoon, I'm good to go for a few more hours." I pulled out my phone and used Google Search. "There's a nightclub not too far from here."

"That sounds like fun."

"Wow. It says they don't close until four in the morning."

I looked up at Sloan. "What do you think? It's our last full night here." Our flight would leave at eight thirty the following night. "If we're going to go out, we need to do it tonight."

She grinned. "Let's do it. After all, I've never been to a Hawaiian nightclub." She shook her glass. "And I could also use some more wine."

I laughed and signaled our server to come over, so I could pay the bill. Ten minutes later, Sloan and I were off for some nightlife fun.

I moved up close behind Sloan and wrapped an arm around her waist while I took a long pull of my beer. I had needed something with less alcohol after Sloan and I did three shots in a row.

Sloan rotated her hips back against me, making me hard. She'd done something similar last night when I put her on all fours and took her from behind.

My tough Sloan, who put up a wall against men, loved sex. Some days, I didn't know how I had gotten to be the lucky fucker who got to make her come every night.

Sloan draped her arm over the back of my neck and kissed my jaw. I pulled her tighter against me, so she could feel my erection.

She smiled and turned in my arms. Her hand slid in between our bodies, and she cupped me over my shorts. My cock jumped against her palm, and she sucked on my neck.

"Baby, you are going to be the death of me," I told her, trying to keep my eyes off her sexy body.

I looked at my watch. It was getting close to closing time. I couldn't wait to take this woman back to our hotel and do dirty things to her. For now, I glided my arm up her waist and brushed my thumb over her nipple.

She pushed her chest out to get closer to my hand, not caring that we were on the dance floor.

The irony was that the club was crowded, but even though there were so many people here, we were all packed in so much that no one noticed or cared what the people next to them were doing. Fifty feet away, another couple was making out. Of course, the copious amounts of alcohol could also be the reason people didn't care what was happening by them.

"I want you to fuck me," Sloan said in my ear.

I groaned. "God, I want that, too." I took another sip of my beer. The sooner I finished it, the sooner I could put both hands all over Sloan.

I handed it to her, and she put her head back and took a long drink.

Her pale throat looked enticing under the lights of the dance floor.

Who knew just her throat would do it for me?

My eyes looked to her hand where my ring sat, and it only made me want her more.

I leaned down next to her ear. "Is it horrible of me to tell you that blackmailing you was the best decision I ever made?"

Sloan nudged the guy next to her. He turned around with a questioning look on his face. "Here, you can have this," she said, pushing the beer toward him.

The guy shrugged, took the bottle, and turned back around to his dance partner.

Sloan shook out her hair and looked up at me. "I'm glad you blackmailed me, too," she said.

I kissed her long and deep. Her slick tongue brushed against mine, and I immediately wanted more. I had no idea how long we would have kissed, but someone bumped into us, knocking us away from each other.

We were both breathing heavy.

"I should've held out for more dates," I said in a low voice.

"What?"

I leaned down to her ear. "I should've held out for more dates." I kissed and sucked on her neck. "I'm not ready to be done with you yet."

She nuzzled me with her nose. "You know, if we got married, we definitely wouldn't be done with each other."

I froze in her arms and slowly pulled back to look at her face.

She tried to smile. "I was joking. I didn't mean to freak—"

"Let's do it."

She laughed in disbelief. "Are you serious?"

"Unless you don't want to."

She bit her lip.

"Fuck that. I don't care if you were joking. Let's do it. I want to marry you."

"Are you for real?"

"Yeah, baby." Because I knew that I didn't want just one more date with this woman. I wanted a hundred more.

THIRTY
SLOAN

CALEB and I left the club right before they kicked everyone out for the night and used his phone to fill out our wedding license. As we hit the Submit button, my head began to spin. Maybe a little from alcohol and maybe a little from our crazy decision.

But then Caleb leaned over and kissed me, and I didn't care how insane our decision was. I wanted to kiss this man forever.

While there was no waiting period to get married in Hawaii, it also wasn't Vegas where they had drive-up wedding chapels. Also, we had to meet with a license agent before we could get married.

With a quick search on the internet, we discovered that our hotel had its own agent, and after some convincing, we got the person to come to work early. I would have never been that bold or demanding, and I didn't think Caleb would have been either, but the two of us were still full of liquid courage.

We finished meeting with the agent, but the wedding

planner told us that they were booked for the day. We told her we didn't care about a big ceremony. We didn't need to include guests, although a fleeting thought of Mary and Ted went through my brain. But I felt like so many things between Caleb and me had been a show for them. I wanted this wedding to be just ours. We didn't need anyone else at our wedding.

It also helped that we still had alcohol in our systems, making us care a bit less if Mary and Ted would be mad at us.

Caleb and I ended up saying *I do* on the beach as the sun rose. It was the officiant, the wedding planner, and the two of us. The hotel had cheap sterling silver rings. We purchased one for Caleb, and I already had the one he'd given me. We slipped the rings on each other's fingers as the officiant announced us as husband and wife.

As Caleb pulled me into his arms and kissed me, a tear escaped my eye.

He pulled back and brushed his thumb over my cheek. "This is going to be a great story to tell our grandkids someday."

I laughed and kissed him again.

The wedding planner handed us a clipboard to sign the marriage certificate, and it was officially official.

I looked up into my husband's eyes and grinned. "We did it."

"Hell yeah, we did." He looked at the planner. "Do you need anything else from us?"

She smiled. "Nope. Go and celebrate your wedding night—or rather, your wedding day."

Caleb grabbed my hand, and we ran toward our hotel.

It felt like it took hours to get up to our floor, and as soon as the elevator doors opened, we ran down the hall.

The wedding planner had found a cheap bouquet for me, which I put to my nose to smell while Caleb opened our door. He pulled me inside and threw the flowers on the bed.

"Hey, I want to save—"

Caleb shut me up with a kiss, and I forgot all about my bouquet.

"Mmm," I said against his mouth as his tongue teased my mouth open.

As he kissed me, he pulled the straps of my dress down. When it landed at my feet, I kicked it off and helped him remove my bra and panties.

Caleb stepped back and drank in the sight of me. The heat in his eyes was intoxicating.

"I can't believe you're mine." He looked up to my eyes. "Do you know all the things I want to do to you?"

I shook my head. "Have you been hiding a kinky side, Mr. Stanton?" I teased.

He laughed. "Nothing you don't already know about me, *Mrs. Stanton.*"

I closed my eyes and sucked in a breath. "Say it again."

He ran his hands along the backs of my thighs and squeezed my ass. "I want to take you bare, Mrs. Stanton," he said against my lips. "I want to feel every inch of you with nothing in between us."

He was making statements, but I knew he was asking for my permission. After Melanie and Neil's situation, the two of us had talked about STIs, and I was on the pill. We could have had sex without a condom weeks ago, but for me, that was something special, and Caleb knew it.

I opened my eyes. "I want that, too. I want to feel you inside me."

Caleb groaned. "You're going to be the death of me."

He'd said that earlier at the club, so he must have really felt it.

"At least you'll die happy," I said.

"Fuck yeah, I will." He glided his hand between my legs and pressed a finger into me. "This is worth dying for." He kissed me and pushed his thumb against my clit. "You're worth dying for."

I pushed him away, and he looked startled.

I laughed. "I don't want to come like that. I want to come with you deep inside me."

He grinned. "I love your sexy mouth."

Caleb pulled me into his arms and picked me up. He carried me over to the bed, and the two of us fell onto it.

"You're wearing too many clothes," I complained.

He stood at the end of the bed and pulled off his shirt. I didn't know if I would ever get sick of seeing Caleb without clothes. His shorts hung low, showing off his impressive V.

"Someday, you're going to have to let me take pictures of you like that," I told him.

He paused as he reached for his pants. "Why?"

"So, I can look at them when you're not around."

He grinned and pushed his shorts and boxers off. "You don't need pictures of me when I'm right here." He put a knee on the bed and crawled up to me, settling between my legs. His cock nudged my entrance. Caleb cursed and shook his head.

"What's wrong?"

"I'm never going to last."

I laughed. "I won't hold it against you."

"*I'll* hold it against me," he said as he scooted down to the end of the bed. "I'm not some teenage boy. I'm a man. And a man should know how to please his partner."

"If you come back up here, I promise I'll be very pleased."

Caleb nudged my thighs apart. "Open. I want to see your pretty pussy."

I spread my legs. "That's an oxymoron."

His gaze was focused on my bottom half as he brushed a finger over my cleft. "What's an oxymoron?" he asked, not looking up.

"Pretty pussy." I sucked in a breath and arched my back as he pressed a finger into me and hooked it on my G-spot.

Caleb looked up at me. "Not when it comes to yours. You have the prettiest damn pussy I've ever seen." The corner of his mouth tilted up. "And I've seen a lot."

"Uh … I don't want to hear about you with other women."

He grinned. "I'm talking about porn. You're the only woman I've been with." His mouth lowered, and he flicked his tongue over my clit.

I knew he was joking, but it sure made me hot to think I was the only woman who'd gotten to make love to him. I supposed I was the only one who would get to do that from now on since we were married.

"Holy shit, baby. You just got wetter. What are you thinking about up there?"

I put my hands on my breasts and tweaked my nipples. "You," I said.

He groaned and proceeded to get me off.

THIRTY-ONE
CALEB

SLOAN'S BACK ARCHED, and she called out my name as her orgasm shook her body. I lifted my head, satisfied with my results, and crawled back up to her. I sat back on my knees between her legs because I wanted to watch as I pushed in raw for the first time.

I hadn't had sex without a condom since the one time in high school with my ex. My cock was so excited; I was worried I was going to embarrass myself.

I rubbed the wetness from Sloan's orgasm onto my eager dick as lube. Not that we needed it, but I liked having a part of her on me.

"Hey, Sloan," I said.

"Huh?" she said in a daze, her eyes at half-mast.

I grinned. "I want you to watch me as I take you bare for the first time."

Her eyes flared.

That's my girl.

I hoped she came again. Maybe I shouldn't have gone down on her.

Although this wouldn't be the last time we did this tonight. I looked at the window where a sliver of sun peeked through. Or this wouldn't be the last time we did this *this morning*. I was still buzzing and not ready for sleep yet.

I still had my hand on my cock, so I leaned forward and rubbed my head against her pussy lips. Then, I slowly pushed the crown in.

I sucked in my breath and bit my lip to keep from shouting.

I looked up into Sloan's eyes and gradually pushed the rest of the way inside her body. "Fuck me," I whispered.

She feels fucking incredible.

I withdrew slowly and thrust in again.

Sloan's hands were on her breasts, and I wanted my mouth there. I leaned over and nudged a hand out of the way, so I could suck on her pink nipple. She cried out, and her core clenched around me.

I increased my strokes and brought my lips up to hers. She slanted her mouth over mine and sucked my tongue into her mouth. By this time, I was pounding into her, wanting to get as deep as I could go, and Sloan widened her legs to let me.

It was so sexy, how she let me have it all.

I ripped my mouth away. "I'm going to come."

"Me, too."

Kissing her on the neck, I said, "You first. I want to feel it."

No sooner had the words left my tongue than she was coming again. Her pussy grabbed on to my cock, and I saw stars. I drove into her as far as I could and exploded, draining myself inside her.

A pounding on the door woke me up. A pounding in my head made me want to go back to sleep.

"Go away," I muttered too low for anyone but Sloan, who was sleeping beside me, to hear.

More pounding sounded.

Sloan leaned back and elbowed me. "Get the door."

"Why me?"

"Because they said your name."

Huh?

"They did?"

"Caleb!" It was Ted.

I sighed and reluctantly got out of bed.

"What is the emergency?" I said, opening the door.

"We have to get to the airport."

I frowned. "But we don't leave until eight thirty."

"Son, it's already six. We need to get going. We have to turn in the rental car and get through security."

I picked up my arm, but my wrist was blurry. My watch finally came into focus, and it indeed was a few minutes after six in the evening. "Crap."

"What the hell did you two do last night?"

I ran my hand down my face and tried to recall the evening. "We went to dinner at the restaurant you'd told us about. Great food, by the way. Then, Sloan and I went to a local nightclub and closed the place down. And then we …"

"Got married?" Ted supplied.

"Holy shit," I whispered. I looked at Ted. "How did you know?"

"You're wearing a wedding ring."

I picked up my hand again and stared at the thin piece of silver on my third finger. "Holy shit."

Ted raised his eyebrows and shook his head. "Congratulations, Caleb. How about you go wake up your new wife, so we can get going?"

Going home was awkward. Ted was unhappy that we'd gotten married like we had, and Mary had cried when she found out she hadn't been invited. Sloan had barely said anything to me since I got her out of bed.

At first, I had been worried that she was freaking out about not making it to the airport in time, but after we made it with plenty of time, I knew she was freaking out about our little impromptu ceremony. And she clearly didn't want to talk about it. But I couldn't blame her. I didn't really want to either. I was still hungover and was in no mood to talk about our future. I had used all my energy getting to the airport and making our connecting flight in Los Angeles.

Hawaii had made everything seem romantic, but now, the reality of heading home was upon us, making everything feel way more substantial. I had no idea what we were supposed to do now.

Stay married? Get divorced? Get an annulment? Try to slow things down and maybe date for real?

I had no clue, and I didn't want to think about it at the moment.

My parents were going to freak. My friends were going to freak. I hadn't even told them I was dating someone, and then I was coming home from a vacation, *married*. They were going to think I was crazy.

I looked over at Sloan. I wondered if her family even knew I existed.

She had big sunglasses on her face even though it was night out and the lights were off in the cabin.

I had offered my shoulder—which she had happily slept on, on the way to Hawaii—but she had told me, "No, thanks," in a voice clearly absent of all appreciation.

I put my head back on the seat and closed my eyes. Despite all the worry, I fell asleep and didn't wake up again until Sloan nudged me. We didn't talk as we got off the plane or as we waited for our luggage, but it was time to go find my car in long-term parking.

Ted and Mary hugged us good-bye. They were still upset, but I could tell they would both come around.

As I pulled out of the parking garage, I finally spoke, "Do you want to come to my place tonight?"

Sloan didn't answer at first. "I think I'm going to head home. Alone. I need to think about some things."

I secretly breathed a sigh of relief that I hadn't known I was holding. I'd had no idea how much I wanted to go back to my apartment by myself until she said something. I needed some familiar ground. I needed time to process.

"Is that okay?" she asked when I didn't answer.

I picked my hand up to put on hers but set it back down. "Of course. We'll talk tomorrow. After we both get some sleep."

Sloan smiled. At that moment, I thought everything might turn out okay, no matter what we decided to do.

THIRTY-TWO
SLOAN

I WALKED into the restaurant right as the hostess called Melanie's name. We quickly hugged each other before following the lady to our table.

"Can I get you anything to drink?" the hostess asked.

"I'll have a wine," Melanie said.

The woman looked at me.

"Water for me, thanks." I was staying away from alcohol for a while.

The hostess left, and I turned to Mel. I'd just returned from Hawaii the night before; I'd promised to meet up with my dear friend to tell her all about it.

"Are those new earrings?" I asked after spotting the beautiful, dangly purple accessories.

She hit one of them with her finger to make it move. "Yes. I bought them with my fifty bucks."

"I thought you were going to buy shoes?"

"I was. But then I saw these babies, and I had to get them."

"Good choice."

"I know." She grinned. "I should have upped the bet to a hundred."

"Never would have happened."

"Because you knew you couldn't keep your hands off of Caleb."

I narrowed my eyes. "I didn't have to tell you I'd slept with him again. I could have kept my money."

Melanie held up her hands. "Hey, I'm only teasing you. I thought you'd be in a better mood after going to Hawaii for almost a week."

She was right. I was testy, and she didn't deserve my wrath.

Our server came over at that time with our drinks. "Do you still need a minute to look at the menu?" he asked.

"Yes, please," I said, reaching for my water glass.

Melanie didn't say anything, so the waiter turned and left. I looked up from my menu to see my friend staring at me.

"What's wrong?"

"What the hell is on your finger?"

I looked down at my left hand and quickly tucked it under the table.

"Sloan Margaret Zehler, did you get engaged? And you didn't tell me? You never said that putting a ring on your finger was part of your deal with Caleb." She made a *come here* motion. "Let me see it."

I reluctantly put my hand on the table, so she could see.

"Ah …" Her eyes got soft. "It's the kind of ring you've always wanted."

"I know." I couldn't help but smile.

"How did this come about? Did he spring it on you?"

"Kind of," I answered. "We were out for breakfast at our hotel, and he went up to get the ring. He texted me on the way back down, saying that Ted had encouraged him to buy it and pop the question. I think he waited because he'd been trying to get out of it."

"I bet that made Ted and Mary happy."

"They were very happy."

Melanie let go of my hand and sat back. "As long as you didn't get married, it's just as easy to break off an engagement as it is a relationship."

I bit the side of my lip.

Melanie leaned forward and shouted, "*You got married?*"

Several tables full of people turned around to look at us.

I smiled awkwardly and leaned forward. "Shh."

"Don't tell me to *shh*. You fucking married Caleb?" She covered her face with her hands. "Why?" She pulled her hands away. "What did he promise you? I think his boss would have been just as happy without you getting married."

"Nothing."

"Nothing what?"

"He didn't promise me anything. Mary and Ted weren't even there."

Melanie's eyes got so big that I thought they were going to pop. "Then, why—what were you—I don't get it."

"Promise not to judge?"

"Sweetie, that ship has sailed. But I promise to support you, no matter what."

"You're judging me? When you dated Neil?"

She took a sip of her wine. "Hey. I judged myself for dating Neil. Now, don't change the subject."

I thought back to our vacation. "It was so"—I shrugged —"romantic. We had a lot of fun together."

"And a lot of sex," Melanie piped in.

I smiled wistfully. "That, too. But, seriously, I had a lot of fun, hanging out with him. We did all this stuff together, and we had a great time. And Hawaii"—I sighed—"it is so beautiful and romantic."

Melanie nodded sympathetically. "You felt like it was the two of you in this bubble. In your own little world."

"*Yes.*" That was exactly it.

"So, now what?"

"We got married our last morning there after being out all night. We had stayed up so late that we slept all day until it was time to go to the airport. After I remembered, I felt stupid and could hardly face him. I don't know Caleb that well, but what if he's regretting the whole thing?"

"Are you regretting the whole thing?"

I stuck out my bottom lip. "I have no idea. I don't know what to think, how to act, or what to do."

"What happened when you got home last night? Did he go to your place, or did you go to his?"

"Neither. We each went to our own places. I needed time to think, and even though he tried to hide it, I could tell Caleb was relieved."

"Have you talked to him today?"

"We exchanged a couple of texts, but they were very casual. I think he's avoiding it as much as I am."

"Do you want to see him?"

"Yes, and no."

Melanie's eyes filled with compassion.

I shook my head. "I don't want to talk about it anymore."

So what if Caleb and I avoided each other for a couple of days? It wouldn't last forever. Eventually, we'd have to talk about it.

"Tell me what you did while I was gone." I wanted to ask about Neil, but I knew she was sick of being babied.

Mel smiled shyly. "I kind of met someone."

"What? That's great."

"Is it? I didn't break up with Neil that long ago."

"Mel, you deserve to find someone who makes you happy."

"Thanks. But I think I'm going to take it slow."

"Slow is a good thing."

"Yeah, we're probably not going to run off and get married."

"Hardy-har-har," I said and unrolled my silverware, so I could throw my napkin at my friend.

Melanie was laughing. "I'm sorry. I couldn't resist."

"What's his name?"

"Justin." She threw my napkin back at me. "But I do want to take it slow before I tell him about the little present Neil left me."

Now, it was my turn to feel sympathetic. "Oh, hon, you don't have to tell him right away. You had a bacterial infection. You took antibiotics. It's gone now. You can't pass it on to him."

I hated Neil for making my friend feel self-conscious about herself. How he and Caleb were brothers was beyond me.

She looked unsure.

"You really don't have to tell him ever. I think you should someday if you get serious. Not because he has to worry about catching anything, but because he should know what Neil did to you." I smiled. "Maybe Justin will kick his ass for you."

A snort-laugh escaped from Mel's mouth. "That's so romantic. I've never had a guy commit a felony for me before," she said sarcastically.

"Sure you did. Caleb punched Neil for you."

Melanie tilted her head. "Let's be real. Caleb punched Neil for *you*."

I couldn't help but smile.

"Promise me something."

"I'll try," I said because I had a feeling that I might not like it.

"If Caleb doesn't reach out to you, you will to him. Because I know you like him, and he likes you."

I nodded. "I promise. But not tonight. Today, I simply want to have dinner with my best friend."

Mel smiled and raised her glass. "Cheers to that."

THIRTY-THREE
CALEB

"WHAT THE FUCK did you just say, dude?"

I sighed at my friend Blake's question.

"He said he got married," Griffin said next to him.

Blake gave Griffin a dirty look. "I heard him, you asshole. That was me expressing my immense displeasure at hearing those words."

"Only you would say 'what the fuck' in one sentence and 'immense displeasure' in the next."

"Boys, can we focus on my problem, please?"

I had called up two of my friends to meet me tonight at Griffin's bar. I needed a drink and some perspective. I was afraid that I might be leaving with only one of those things.

Blake and Griffin turned to me.

"You're so selfish," Blake said sarcastically.

"Yeah. Marriage has turned you into a needy pussy," Griffin joked.

I rolled my eyes. "I don't know why I'm friends with either of you."

"It's because I give good head," Blake said.

"Except you've never offered to do that for me, so that can't be it," I said dryly.

"Is that giving head to men or women?" Griffin asked.

"Both."

"You can't be good at both."

"The hell I can't."

"Bullshit. I don't believe you."

Blake smiled and raised his glass to his lips. "I could put you in touch with the couple I had a threesome with last night."

I sighed and grabbed my wallet. I opened it up and counted a few bills.

"What are you doing?" Griffin asked.

"Leaving money to cover my beer." I didn't feel like listening to my friends fight or hearing about another one of Blake's threesomes.

I should have never called him. The guy only screwed couples, so he didn't have to commit to anyone. I couldn't imagine what kind of advice he was going to offer me.

"Come on, man. Don't leave," Griffin said, as his best friend, Madeline, walked into the bar and over to us.

I raised an eyebrow.

"I promise to listen," he said.

"Me too," Madeline said as she sat down at the table.

It wouldn't hurt to get a female perspective.

I looked at Blake, who said nothing.

Griffin elbowed him in the ribs.

"Fine," Blake said. "I will listen, too."

I wasn't sure if I believed him, but when Blake picked up my money and threw it at me, I relented.

"Start at the beginning," Blake said. "How the hell did you even get engaged without us knowing this girl?"

"*You got engaged?*" Madeline asked, shocked.

If I was going to tell them everything, I needed another beer. I lifted my arm to signal the waitress before launching into my story.

When I finished, I had to give my two male buddies credit. They'd listened to the whole thing, only interrupting me a few times to ask questions. I realized that was why I'd called the two of them. They could be reliable when I really needed them to be.

Blake whistled. "Why didn't you tell us you might not get the store?"

I shrugged. "I didn't want to admit it, I guess."

"But you told Sloan."

"Only because I had to. And, at the time, I barely knew her. She didn't count."

None of them noticed my use of the past tense.

"That's bullshit that Ted is actually thinking of selling the store to someone else. You've worked your ass off for him for years. That store should be yours," Blake said.

"Thanks, man."

"So, you started this to show Ted you could settle down. Has he said any more about who he's going to sell to?" Griffin asked.

"Not a peep. And I haven't asked him." I took a drink. "And, now, he's disappointed in me."

"What the fuck for?" Blake asked.

"Because Sloan and I got married."

Griffin held up a hand. "Wait. I thought he wanted you to get married."

"He did. I think he was just disappointed that we'd gotten married without him and Mary there."

"That doesn't seem right to me," Griffin said.

I shrugged. "He did pay for the trip. And Mary cried when she found out. They weren't all happy tears either. He's not happy that I hurt Mary's feelings."

"Are you sure Ted and Mary aren't your real parents?" Blake asked.

I laughed. "I know. Sometimes, I feel like I am closer to them. Or just as close."

"That's why you should get to buy the store."

Nodding my agreement, I took a long drink.

"What are you going to do about your wife?" Griffin asked.

"That sounds so weird," Blake said. "Caleb's wife."

"Imagine how I feel," I said.

Blake leaned forward and smirked. "I know you said you did it because you were both drunk, but tell me you did it a little for the pussy, too. She must really know how to ride the dick."

I leaned forward like I was ready to kiss and tell, but I turned my smile into a scowl. "You ever talk about Sloan that way again, I will chop off your balls and shove them up your ass, and then you'll become the reigning champion of giving head because it'll be the only way you're able to have sex."

Blake leaned back and burst into laughter. "You are in so much trouble." He shook his head like he felt sorry for me.

"You're an asshole."

Blake opened his mouth, but Griffin elbowed him again

205

before he could say anything. "I think that Blake is trying to say that it's obvious that you like this Sloan."

"I agree with Griff," Madeline said.

"I do," I admitted. "That's why I don't know what to do."

"Because you don't want to be married?" Griffin asked.

I thought about it. "Because I don't know if I want to be married," I corrected.

"Do you have to decide today?" Madeline asked.

"Yeah," Griffin said, "do you have to decide today? What's going to happen if you wait?"

I had no idea.

"It sounds like Sloan isn't beating down your door and calling you every five minutes for an answer."

"That's true," I said.

"Then, why don't you just wait and see how you feel after a few days? A week? You literally got back from Hawaii less than twenty-four hours ago," Madeline said.

I smiled. "Thanks, guys. And Madeline." I appreciated their advice.

"You're welcome," Blake said. "Now, tell us what Sloan looks like. Is she hot?"

I sighed and shook my head. "Are you always thinking about sex?"

"Duh. That's why I'm bi. I need the option of many, many sexual partners. Women or men alone are not enough."

I looked at Griffin. "Remind me again why we put up with him."

Griffin laughed, and Blake gave me the finger.

An hour later, I knocked on Sloan's front door. It was getting late for a weeknight, and I didn't want to wake her by ringing the doorbell. If she was already sleeping, I knew that meant I was supposed to go home.

When a couple of loud barks sounded from inside the house, I cursed myself. I was never getting a dog.

But, as the door opened and a big brown nose stuck out of the crack, I remembered that, since Sloan and I were married, I technically already did have one.

The door opened all the way, and there my wife—*my wife!*—stood on the other side of the threshold. She looked as uncertain and nervous as I felt. But she was also in her pajamas, and she looked adorable.

I had missed sleeping with her last night.

"Hey," I said.

"Hey."

"I know we need to talk and figure some things out, but tonight, I was hoping that we could put that aside for now."

"Then, why are you here?" she asked.

"I was hoping I could sleep with you."

She opened her mouth, and I put my hand up.

"And, by sleep, I mean, *sleep*. I slept like crap last night." I didn't want to say it was because she hadn't been there, and I hoped she wouldn't ask.

When she stuck out her hand to me, I sighed with relief. Every muscle in my body relaxed.

"Come on, Caleb. Let's go to bed."

THIRTY-FOUR
SLOAN

I LED Caleb to my room and slowly removed his clothes. In Hawaii, he'd either slept naked or in his boxers.

I knew he'd meant it when he said that he was really there to sleep, but I couldn't resist kissing his collarbone and his neck. I pushed off his shorts and was ready to kiss him lower, but he took my hand and brought me over to my bed.

We lay down, and he pulled me into his arms.

When my nose was firmly tucked under his chin, he whispered, "I missed you last night."

"I missed you, too," I whispered back.

The next morning, I woke up first and stared at Caleb while he slept. He was only thirty-one, but he looked even younger when he was sleeping.

I wondered if most people did because, in sleep, they were free of stress, work, and their never-ending to-do lists.

I looked down at the ring on his hand, and it occurred to

me that this was the first morning of waking up next to my husband. *Eek!* That word still sounded funny in my head.

Technically, we'd woken up in the same bed after our wedding, but we'd both been hungover and rushing to get to the airport on time. Not to mention, we'd both been embarrassed, and we hadn't wanted to face each other.

As much as we needed to talk about things, I was glad we hadn't done it last night.

Caleb's breathing changed, and I realized he was waking up. I looked away from his face, so he wouldn't think I was a creeper.

"Hey," he said, his voice rough from sleep.

I looked up. "Hey."

"How long have you been awake?"

I lifted a shoulder. "Only a few minutes. Not long enough for Bear to insist I let him outside."

Caleb chuckled and looked down at the huge ball of fur sleeping at the end of the bed. "Don't tell Bear, but I kind of missed him, too."

Bear lifted his head at the sound of his name.

"Go back to sleep," Caleb told him.

Not one to take direction easily, Bear got up and walked toward our heads, stopping when he was close enough to lick Caleb's face.

"I think he heard you," I said. "And he wants you to know he missed you, too."

Caleb laughed and pushed Bear away. "Not the mouth, man."

Bear lay down and put his head on Caleb's chest.

Caleb rubbed Bear's head as awkwardness began to set in.

"I guess we should talk about it, huh?" I said.

"I suppose."

"Let's start at the beginning then. We did a thing. A kind of crazy thing."

Caleb chuckled. "Kind of crazy? Full-on crazy."

Hearing him say that made me a little sad even if he was right. "Okay, full-on crazy. Now, what do we do?"

"What do you want to do?" he asked.

"Oh, sure, throw the question back at me."

He grinned. "What if I told you there was no right or wrong answer?"

I took a deep breath. "That helps." I looked up into his eyes. "What if I told you I didn't know what I wanted to do?"

He reached for my hand and brought it up to his mouth to kiss it. "I'd tell you I felt the same."

I was relieved and still a little disappointed. The pressure was off to make things work, but it would have been nice to know that he really wanted to stay married to me.

This was why getting involved with someone was a bad idea. They made you feel all sorts of things.

Caleb squeezed my hand. "Hey, you."

"What?"

"Where did you go?"

"Just thinking, I guess."

"Can I tell you what I do know?" he asked.

"Of course."

"I know that I like being with you, and I don't want us to break up." He tilted his head. "Can we even break up if we're not officially dating?"

I smiled. "Good question." I bit my lip. "What if we

start officially dating and put the marriage thing on the back burner? Pretend like it hasn't happened until we know more?" I pulled off the ring from my left hand and put it on my right.

Caleb did the same. "Except around Mary and Ted," he reminded me.

"Right."

I had to admit, I was getting sick of the ruse. Sure, it was easier now that Caleb and I had decided to officially date, but we'd had to go and add another complication. We could tell everyone we were dating, but Mary and Ted knew we were married. It was like we were leading double lives. And, now, if things didn't work out, we couldn't break up; we'd have to get a divorce.

I threw an arm over my eyes. "Why did we have to make things so complicated?"

"Bear, go," Caleb said.

I felt the bed move as my dog jumped off, and Caleb turned toward me.

He pulled my arm away and looked down at me. "Let's just take things one day at a time. We don't have to decide anything today. And we don't even have plans to see Ted and Mary anytime soon. Let's just relax and enjoy each other."

"You're pretty wise," I told him.

"I would like to say it's all me, but I got some advice from my friends last night."

I gasped mockingly. "You have friends?"

He rolled his eyes but smiled. "Yes, I have friends."

"Do I get to meet them?" I held my breath, waiting to see how he'd answer. If he told me no, then I'd have to wonder if he was serious about being with me or if he was keeping me around for the stupid store.

"Yes," he said hesitantly.

My hopes deflated, but I was determined to stay strong and act like it was no big deal. "I understand."

He frowned. "No, you don't. Get whatever negative thought you have going on in your head out."

Now, I frowned. *How does he know me so well?*

"I'm not a hundred percent on board because my friends … are a little crass. You might change your mind about me."

I grinned despite trying not to. "I can handle crass. I hang out with you, don't I?"

"Full of jokes this morning, aren't you?"

I shrugged. "I can't help that I'm so funny."

Caleb snorted and rolled away to sit up. "I said you were full of jokes. I did not say you were funny."

"*Hey.*"

He laughed and turned back around to me. "You want to meet my friends. What about my parents?"

"I've already met your parents."

He rolled his eyes again. "As my girlfriend. How would you like to meet them as my girlfriend?"

I smiled. "Okay. When?"

"Tonight."

THIRTY-FIVE
CALEB

"HOW LONG HAVE the two of you been dating?" my mom asked.

Shit.

Sloan and I hadn't even considered talking about this stuff before we came over tonight. The two of us and my mother were sitting in my parents' backyard, having a beer, while we waited for my dad to get home, so we could have dinner.

"About a month," Sloan said. "We started dating after the night I picked Melanie up from here."

My mom's eyes turned gloomy. "I was sad to hear about the two of them breaking up."

"Yes, it was sad," Sloan agreed.

I couldn't help but snort behind my beer bottle. Sloan was anything but sad about the two of them calling it quits.

She kicked me under the table.

"Melanie was always such a polite girl, and I always thought Neil could have treated her better."

This surprised me. "Really?"

"Caleb, just because I'm a mother doesn't mean I'm blind. Your brother let his ambition get to him, I think, which is sad because I think Melanie was good for him."

She might have been good for him, but he hadn't been good for her.

My mom leaned forward and lowered her voice even though we were the only people in the backyard. "Neil started going to therapy."

"You're shitting me," I said.

When I'd suggested my brother talk to someone about his chronic cheating, I'd never thought he'd listen to me.

"Caleb, no swearing."

"Sorry."

"But yes, your brother is seeing someone. He told me he needed to figure some stuff out after his breakup with Melanie."

I looked over at Sloan. She looked as stunned as I felt.

"That's great," Sloan said.

"Please don't tell Melanie," my mother said. "I shouldn't have said anything."

"I won't say anything," Sloan promised.

Yeah, right. She was going to tell Melanie the minute we left the house.

"Anyway, you're also the one who helped Caleb find his house, correct?" my mom asked.

"Yep. That's kind of how we started dating."

My mom smiled. "That's quite the love story."

"Sure is," I said.

"When do you close?" my mom asked.

"Next month." I didn't know the exact date. That was what Sloan was for.

My mom shook her head in amazement. "I'm so happy. I didn't think you'd ever settle down."

"Mom, Sloan and I just started dating. It's not like we're getting married."

Sloan started coughing next to me and put her own beer down.

I massaged her on the back. I probably should have made sure she wasn't taking a drink when I said the marriage line.

"I know," my mother said as if I'd called her dumb. "It's the house, too. I was always afraid you'd move away."

I frowned. *Why does everyone think that?* First, Ted, and now, my mom.

"I lived in Europe for one year, ten years ago. I wasn't planning to go back."

She patted my leg. "I know, honey."

I hated it when she patronized me.

I threw a hand up in defeat, and Sloan laughed beside me.

"Oh, there's your father," my mom said as I heard the sounds of someone in the kitchen. "I'd better go and help get dinner started." She stood.

"I'll help," Sloan said, following my mother.

I figured I might as well help, too. We could make it a family affair.

My dad was unloading the groceries when we walked in. "Hey, Caleb. Hello, Sloan."

"Hey, Dad."

He smiled. "So, this is your new girlfriend?"

Sloan smiled shyly.

I put my arm around her. "Yep."

"I'm glad to know you're actually dating someone because I just had the strangest conversation at Home Depot."

A sinking feeling landed in my stomach. I didn't want to know, but I had to ask, "Oh?"

"Yeah, I ran into Ted."

I swallowed over the lump forming in my throat. "Oh?"

Ted and Mary lived on the opposite side of the Cities. My Dad and Ted should have never been in the same store.

"Yeah. I almost didn't recognize him at first, but then I realized it's probably been about three to four years since I saw him. And I haven't been to the store in ages."

I was getting more nervous by the minute, and Sloan squeezed my side. I wished my father would just spit out what they had talked about.

"Yeah, I suppose it's been a long time," I said. Something I had been counting on since this whole charade started.

"Anyway, he was under the impression that you two had been dating for a long time and that the two of you got married in Hawaii." My father threw his head back and laughed. "I thought the whole thing was ridiculous. I had to tell him that you were bringing Sloan over for the first time tonight."

My mother, who had been pulling stuff from the cupboards and fridge, turned around, looking confused. "Hawaii?" She looked from Sloan to me. "You didn't tell us that Sloan went to Hawaii with you."

Of course I didn't. It would have been too much to explain. And, now, I didn't know if I should deny it or tell them the truth.

"I did go," Sloan said before I could make a decision. "Ted and Mary were kind enough to let me come with."

After she said it, I knew it was a mistake because my mother was going to hone in on the other thing my dad had said.

"So, why does Ted think you two got married?"

And there it was. I knew my mother wouldn't forget what she'd heard.

My father waved his hand in the air before either Sloan or me could answer. "I told Ted it had to be a joke since the two of you haven't been dating long. I told him that, just last month, Sloan had been here and that you two had exchanged phone numbers, so Sloan could start showing you houses."

The blood drained from my face because Ted wasn't going to think I was playing a joke on him. He was going to think I'd lied. Which, in all fairness, I had. But Sloan and I really had gotten married. That part was the truth.

I dropped my arm from Sloan's shoulders. "I need to go."

"Caleb, you never answered the question," my mom said, bringing out her *I mean business* voice. "Was it a joke, or are the two of you married?"

Caught in one lie, I really didn't feel like telling another. I stepped around to my mother and put my hands on her shoulders. "I don't have time to talk about this right now. I need to find Ted. Don't wait for me. I probably won't be back." I kissed her on the forehead and walked away. I snagged my keys from the counter and headed for the door.

I needed to talk to Ted. Now.

THIRTY-SIX
SLOAN

CALEB'S PARENTS looked confused as Caleb walked outside to his car. I knew they wanted an explanation, but it wasn't mine to give.

I set my beer down. "Thank you for everything, but I'd better go with him." I took off running toward the door.

"Sloan, wait," his mother called out.

"I have to go. I'm sorry," I said as I ran out the door. "Wait for me," I yelled to Caleb.

I knew he was in a hurry, but he really couldn't go over there without me.

As soon as I shut the door, Caleb sped out of the driveway and down the street.

I tried to talk to Caleb on the way over to Ted's, but he was sort of stuck in a loop in his own mind.

He kept saying over and over, "I should have told him sooner. I should have told him sooner."

I started to feel bad since I was the one who'd told him not to do it.

Needless to say, it was a long drive.

When we arrived, Caleb got out and went right to the door. Once again, I had to chase after him. I knew he was stressed and anxious, but if he let me, I would stand by his side and share responsibility for what had happened.

Mary opened the door right as I reached him. She looked at the two of us and shook her head. The disappointment in her eyes was like a punch in the gut. And, until that moment, I didn't realize how much I had come to like her.

"Is Ted here?"

"He's in the study," she said, but she didn't move out of the way.

"Can I speak to him?"

"Why did you lie, Caleb?" Her eyes glanced my way, and I knew the question was for me, too.

Caleb hung his head. "I didn't want to lose the store."

"Lose the store?" Mary said.

Caleb grimaced, and I could guess what he was thinking. His comment made him sound like a selfish, greedy asshole.

"It's a long story, Mary. I-I need to talk to Ted."

I didn't think it was possible for Mary to show more disappointment, but she looked down at our hands and saw the rings on our right ring fingers. It was written all over her face. She took a step back and swept her arm out.

We entered, and I paused in front of Mary. "I'm sorry. It was never meant to get this far."

"I'm not sure what to think anymore," she said.

"I'm sure Caleb and I will come back and talk to you,

too. But he really wants to speak with Ted first." I nodded in the direction Caleb had gone. "I'd better go."

I set off to help Caleb explain how things had gotten here, but when I reached the study, the door was closed.

I frowned. *Why didn't Caleb wait for me?*

I turned to go back to Mary when I heard the two men talking, and curiosity got the best of me.

"Let me get this straight." It was Ted. "You lied to me about having a girlfriend because you didn't want me to sell the store to Rick."

"When you say it like that, it makes me sound like a selfish prick."

"Aren't you?"

Ouch. That had to hurt.

"No."

Oh, Caleb, you're not, but you need to take some responsibility for your actions.

"I have worked for you since high school. It's the only job I've ever known. But not only that, I also fricking love it. I've put in more than my share of time, and I've offered up more than my share of ideas. I deserve to buy the store," Caleb said. "I thought working for you for that long would show you how committed I was, but then you started going on about nothing tying me down. If you had let me buy the store, the store would have tied me down."

"I see your point, but you still lied to me."

"You're right, and I'm sorry."

"I appreciate your apology, but you understand that I can't possibly sell you the store now, right?"

I put my hand to my mouth and sucked in a breath.

Caleb didn't say anything, but I thought I'd heard a strangled moan come from the other side of the door.

"You lied to me, Caleb," Ted said. "You led me to believe this Sloan was your girlfriend. You let us think you were getting married. You let me pay for the both of you to go to Hawaii."

Tell him, Caleb. Tell him that we're more than just two people who tried to trick him. Tell him we care about each other, I silently begged.

"You lied to me, and you lied to my wife," Ted continued. "Today, when I ran into your father, I was embarrassed. I looked like a fool. It'll be a long time before I can forgive you."

"I understand." Caleb's voice was small.

"I'm not going to fire you because we have a lot of history. Also, you're right; you've done a lot for the store. But I'm not going to sell it to you. And I don't want to see Sloan here or anywhere near the store."

Panic came crushing down on me as a million thoughts swirled around in my brain. Ted hated me. Ted blamed me. Did this mean I could never see Caleb again? And, most of all, was Caleb going to fight for me?

"But—" Caleb said.

"I don't want to hear it. I realize that the both of you are to blame, but I didn't even know the girl, and she was willing to deceive me."

Tell him, Caleb. Tell him how you blackmailed me.

"I understand," were the only things out of his mouth, and I thought my heart broke right then and there.

It was time for me to walk away. I couldn't listen to any more of their conversation.

I slowly walked down the hall and out to the front door. My limbs felt like they weighed a million pounds.

"Are you okay?"

I jumped as I realized that Mary was sitting outside on the porch.

The corner of her mouth tipped up if only for a second. "Sorry."

I stepped closer to Mary as she stood. Now was the time to tell her my side and defend myself to someone. I opened my mouth to tell her how Caleb had forced me to become his girlfriend or send me to jail. But I couldn't do it. Mary loved him. And I thought I did a little bit, too. That was why it hurt so much that he hadn't told Ted the whole story.

"I want you to know that Caleb and I got together for the wrong reasons, but we did come to care about each other. I'm so sorry we lied to you."

Sympathy filled Mary's eyes. "The wedding? The marriage?"

I knew what she was asking. Had we carried our lie that far? Had we faked it? Because we could have easily bought Caleb a ring. They hadn't been there for the wedding.

I shook my head. "The wedding was real. We were a little drunk." Okay, a lot drunk. "But the marriage is real." I looked toward the house. "Or it was real."

"Don't give up on him, dear."

It was sweet that Mary still wanted us to be together.

"I'll try," I said.

But I thought that Caleb had already given up on me.

THIRTY-SEVEN
CALEB

BY THE TIME I left Ted's office, I felt like one hundred percent shit.

I had lied to one of the people I cared about most in the world. And I'd hurt him deeply.

I walked outside to see Sloan and Mary on the porch.

Mary smiled at me, unlike when she'd answered the door, but Sloan wouldn't look at me.

"I'm sorry, Mary. I know I said we'd talk, but do you mind if we do it another time? I need to get Sloan home."

"I'm very disappointed in you, Caleb Stanton. And I'm going to hold you to that conversation."

"Yes, ma'am."

Mary squeezed both our arms and went into the house. I thought she was already halfway to forgiving me, and we hadn't even talked yet.

Ted, on the other hand …

Even though he hadn't fired me, I knew it was probably time for me to start looking for a new job. I had completely blown my chances of buying the store now.

"Let's go," I said to Sloan.

As I followed behind her, a ton of emotions went through me. I was embarrassed that I had gotten caught. I didn't know how to tell her that Ted didn't want her coming around for a while. Even if he hadn't said *a while*, I knew he didn't mean permanently.

But I was also mad at Sloan. It wasn't fair, but I was. I was angry that she'd talked me out of coming clean. If I had told them before Hawaii, things wouldn't have ended up the way they did. I wouldn't look like a freeloader. And neither would Sloan. I couldn't help but place some of the blame on her for putting me in this position.

We drove to her house in silence. It was the most god-awful silence I'd ever endured. And this coming from a guy who had hitchhiked around Europe. Getting a ride from strangers could be weird.

When we got to her house, she opened her door, and I made no move to shut off the car and follow her.

She put a foot on the ground but then turned around and looked at me. "Why didn't you tell Ted that you'd black-mailed me?"

Huh? "What?"

"I heard you. You let Ted think that I was your willing accomplice. Why didn't you tell him?"

"You were eavesdropping?"

"Yeah. Because you shut me out. And don't change the subject. Why didn't you tell him?"

I threw my hands up and rolled my eyes. I was trying not to get pissed, but it was hard. "I am hanging by a thread in this guy's good graces, and you want me to tell him I black-mailed you, too?"

"It's the—"

I cut her off, "Not to mention, I'd have to tell him what I blackmailed you for. You're already on Ted's shit list. How do you think he'd take it that you vandalized my brother's car?"

She closed her mouth.

"Yeah, that's what I thought. And I'm sorry, but I've known Ted and Mary for a lot longer than you have. My relationship is way more important with them than yours is."

She recoiled like I'd slapped her. "I guess I know where I stand."

"What the fuck is that supposed to mean?"

"Being a part of your life, my relationship with them should be just as important as yours."

"That's not what I meant."

"Oh. So, were you going to tell me I'm banned from going to their house and the store?"

"Yes. But you're overreacting. It won't—"

"I'm not overreacting. You didn't stick up for me."

I clenched my jaw and took in a deep breath. It didn't work. "*I* didn't stick up for you? I could have told Ted that I wanted to tell him and Mary the night we got the plane tickets, but *you* talked me out of it. I could have placed the blame all at your feet right there. I could have made it sound like you wanted a free trip out of the deal."

"But that's not true."

"I know it's not. That's why I didn't say it." *Is she purposely being obtuse?* "But you did talk me out of it. If I had told him, we wouldn't be in the mess we are now."

She leaned closer to me and narrowed her eyes. "If you

225

had never blackmailed me, we wouldn't be in the mess we are in now."

"You're right. I suppose we're both to blame."

"I wish I had never agreed to this stupid deal. Jail would have been better than pretending to be your girlfriend."

I rubbed the spot over my heart. I knew she was saying it because she was upset and confused, but damn it if that didn't hurt. This morning, we had talked about giving our relationship a chance, and now, she was saying she wished nothing had ever happened between us.

And, because I didn't want her to know I was hurt, I opened my big mouth and said, "Yeah. Same here. Except I would have missed out on all the great sex."

She shook her head in disgust. "Typical, Caleb. Always making jokes when things get serious."

"What the fuck are you talking about?"

"Nothing. It doesn't matter anyway." She practically ejected herself from the car. "Tell Ted he doesn't have to worry about seeing me."

"Good," I said, not meaning it.

"Good," she said and slammed the door.

I pushed down on the gas pedal before I said something else I knew I'd regret. But, as I drove away, the pit in my stomach that had started at my parents' house was so big that I feared it was going to swallow me whole.

THIRTY-EIGHT

SLOAN

"YOU HAVEN'T HEARD from Caleb yet?" Melanie asked me as we lounged on my couch a week later.

A familiar pain went through me. "Nope. We broke up, remember?"

Out of the corner of my eye, I saw her turn to look at me.

"Did you message him?" she asked, completely ignoring the part where I'd said we broke up.

"Nope."

"You know, one of you has to make the first move."

I shrugged. "No, we don't, but if it's going to be anyone, it should be him."

After he hadn't defended me, I was not going to grovel to him.

"Damn, you're stubborn."

I shrugged. "Maybe." Or maybe I didn't feel like getting my heart broken again. "There's nothing wrong with being single." I wish I had stayed that way. This was why relationships sucked. It always ended badly.

"I'm glad being single is not a negative because I have some news for you."

The way she'd said it had me whipping my head toward her. "What news?"

"I'm pregnant."

"*No way.*" My eyes widened. "Neil's?"

"Yeah," she said with a *what are you going to do* smile.

"I don't know how to react. Are we excited? Are we mad? Are we scared? Are we freaking out?" I gasped. "Oh no. You had wine at the restaurant."

Melanie laughed and grabbed my arm in her hands. "I had one glass of wine. The doctor says it's probably fine. And I love all this *we* talk. This is why I love you."

"You know I'm here for you, no matter what. If you want to go to the clinic, I'm there for you. If you want to give it up for adoption, I'll help you find the best damn parents we can. Or, if you decide to keep it, I'll be the best honorary auntie there is."

Melanie took a deep breath and rubbed her belly. "I was freaked out at first. I've always wanted to be a mom, but I didn't see myself becoming a single mom. And I don't know how I feel about being tied to Neil for the rest of my life, but I'm hoping we can co-parent well together. He actually called me the other day and apologized."

I lifted my brow. "Really?"

"Really. Maybe he truly is going to counseling."

After I had calmed down a bit from my breakup with Caleb, I had remembered to tell Melanie what his mom had said about Neil seeing a therapist.

"As long as you don't get back together with him, I'm all

for you two trying to be friends for the sake of the baby. That is, if you're going to keep it. Have you told him yet?"

Mel shook her head. "You don't have to worry about us getting back together. I sincerely hope he can change and grow, but it's too late for us. And the longer I'm away from him, the more I realize that, while I did love him, I really don't miss him that much. My life is better without him in it."

I wish I felt that way. I missed Caleb like crazy. His jokes, the way he'd held me at night, the way he'd looked at me when he was inside me … I missed it all. Just that morning, I'd reached out for him, only to remember he wasn't there. Again.

"As for keeping the baby," Mel said, "I've decided I'm going to do it."

I whooped for joy. "I get to be an auntie."

Melanie laughed. "But I haven't told Neil yet, so don't say anything to Caleb. I just found out. I want to make it to the second trimester before I spring it on him. In case I lose the pregnancy." She tapped her chin. "Maybe I should find out what days he goes to the counselor, so I can tell him before his appointment. In case he needs the extra therapy."

I laughed. "Your secret is safe with me. I doubt I'll be talking to Caleb anytime soon."

"Aw, babe. You don't know that. And, even if neither one of you admits defeat and contacts the other, don't you have to go to his closing soon?"

I groaned. Caleb was closing on his house in a few weeks, so we'd be forced to see each other.

"Maybe I can get someone else to take over for me."

"Sloan, you might be stubborn, but you're not afraid of confrontation."

"Are you sure?" Because I sure felt like I was.

"You'll go, and you'll talk to him. Everything will be fine."

Everything was not fine. Everything sucked.

It was the day of Caleb's closing, and I went through every article of clothing in my closet. And then I got mad at myself for wanting to look good for him. I would show up in a potato sack, except it would be unprofessional and everyone would stare at me for the wrong reasons.

In the end, I ran through the last five outfits I could remember and picked something similar. I would not go out of my way to impress someone who couldn't even be bothered to apologize.

My phone dinged, and for a second, I got my hopes up, but it was only Mel.

> Melanie: Go with an open mind today. Remember, you haven't apologized either.

> Me: Go away and quit reading my mind.

> Melanie: Ha-haha-haha. Love you and good luck!

> Me: Thanks.

I made sure to arrive early to the closing. I didn't want to do anything embarrassing by walking into the room and then tripping over my own feet at the sight of Caleb there.

I arrived first and made small talk with the seller's realtor and the closing agent. The seller was second to last to arrive, and I began to get nervous that Caleb wasn't going to show.

I should have texted him. Even if we weren't together, I still could have contacted him for professional reasons. Now, it looked like I hadn't out of spite or something.

When Caleb finally breezed through the door at five after, I breathed a sigh of relief.

"Sorry I'm late," he said, taking the open seat next to me.

The closing agent, a middle-aged woman, smiled at him. "It's fine." She looked around the table. "Let's get started then."

Sitting next to Caleb during the process was torture. I could feel the heat from his body and smell the familiar scent of his shampoo. A few times, his thigh brushed mine, and I thought I was going to jump out of my chair. And let's not forget how good he looked. He smiled throughout the closing, looking handsome and refreshed.

He obviously hadn't lost any sleep over me, and pretending like nothing had happened to us was so much harder than I had anticipated. I managed to hold it together and stay professional until the end when Caleb went to sign the few papers.

Both his hands were bare.

I quickly shoved my right hand under the table where I still wore the ring he'd bought me.

That right there showed me how we both felt. I had been acting tough, but I'd been hoping we'd get back together.

Caleb had obviously moved on.

As discreetly as possible, I removed the ring with my hands in my lap and shoved the ring in my pocket. I prayed he hadn't already noticed that I was wearing it.

He probably thought I was a loser.

"Thanks for coming, everyone," the closing agent said. "And congrats on your new house, Mr. Stanton."

Caleb grinned. "Thank you."

The rest of us got up from our seats and made our way out of the building.

Once everyone started breaking off for their cars, Caleb said, "Sloan?"

I sucked in a deep breath and turned to him. "Yeah?"

He nervously looked away. "I just wanted to tell you that I'm sorry."

Despite the apology, I didn't have a good feeling about this.

"I'm sorry I dragged you into my work mess. And I'm sorry I ..." He smiled wistfully. "Well, I'm sorry."

I nodded. "I'm sorry, too."

Caleb sighed with relief. "Good. I was afraid you'd be mad at me forever."

I shook my head. "I could never."

He smiled. "I'm glad."

He looked at his watch, and I shoved my free hand that

wasn't holding my briefcase in my pocket, so I wouldn't be tempted to reach for him.

"Listen, I have to go. But it was nice seeing you again. Thanks for helping me find a great house."

"You're-you're welcome," I managed to say. My fingers played with my ring, and I wondered if I should give it back to him.

Caleb pulled his keys from his pocket and started walking backward. "Thanks again, Sloan. It was good to see you."

"It was nice seeing you, too."

Caleb turned and headed to his truck while I stood there, staring after him.

After he pulled away, I realized I was still playing with the ring, and I was glad I hadn't given it back. It was the last thing I had from him.

I was able to get my feet moving again and made my way to my car. Caleb was happy and had moved on. He and I were truly over.

I cried all the way to my office, and later that night, I went home and filed for an annulment. It was also the day our marriage certificate came in the mail. Life was a fickle bitch.

THIRTY-NINE
CALEB

I STARED down at the papers that had been delivered to me.

Annulment papers.

I sat down at my new dining room table, stunned.

I couldn't believe it. I supposed I shouldn't have been surprised, but I was.

I'd left the ball in Sloan's court, hoping she'd reach out to me. Instead, she served me with annulment papers. They were almost worse than divorce papers because it was like saying our marriage had never happened. It was like saying *we* had never happened.

It was the end of October, and I hadn't seen Sloan for a month now, but I had been busy. Moving took a lot longer and was more effort than I had anticipated. Also, I was working my ass off at the store to get back into Ted's good graces, so a part of me put my relationship with Sloan off to the side. Maybe too much off to the side, as I didn't realize how much time had passed since I last spoke to her.

I thought things were good between us after seeing each

other at the closing on my house. I had almost left without saying anything, but I couldn't just walk away without trying. So, I'd apologized and let her know there were no hard feelings on my side. The way she'd told me that she couldn't stay mad at me gave me hope. Yet my phone didn't ring, and I didn't receive one text from her. I then assumed she needed more time, and I would hear from her when she was ready.

I had not thought I'd hear from her in the form of annulment papers.

And I didn't know how that made me feel.

I missed her like crazy. Seeing her a month ago had made me realize how much I cared about her. But she'd been cold and distant. Much like the Sloan I'd known before our agreement.

I needed time to think, time to process, so I put the papers on my stuff-to-do pile and went out for a run.

───────

A few days later, there was a knock at my door. I was surprised to see my brother standing on my front steps.

"Hi."

"Hey," I said.

"Do you mind if I come in?"

"Uh, no." I turned around, so Neil could follow me into the house. "Sorry for the mess. I've been slowly unpacking. Now that I have a bigger place to live, Mom and Dad brought over old boxes of my stuff they'd had in the basement. It's been a process."

"You'll get there."

I raised my brow at his words of support. I'd expected him to tell me to hire someone to take care of my mess.

"What's up?" I asked because my brother had never come over just to visit me.

The two of us had never been close. Well, maybe when we were kids, but even back then, we'd been interested in different things. I always liked sports, which made my job all the more fun. Neil was always interested in other things. I remembered him playing a lot of video games on the computer.

But even though we'd never been close, he hadn't always been an asshole either. Sure, he'd never been faithful to a girlfriend, but the way he'd treated Melanie was a newer thing.

Neil took a deep breath. "I came here to tell you thank you."

Whoa. That was unexpected.

"For what?"

He pointed to my couch. "Do you mind if I sit?"

I shook my head. "Be my guest."

We took seats on opposite ends.

"That night you came and got me from Mel's house, you told me to go and talk to someone."

"Oh, yeah, Mom said you'd been doing that."

"And, if you hadn't pushed me in that direction, I don't know that I would have."

"I'm glad you did. Honestly, you were so drunk that I didn't think you'd even remember our conversation."

Neil smiled. "I was drunk, but it did come back to me in pieces. Especially the part about how I would feel if I found out Melanie had cheated on me." He shook his head in amazement. "I was a real ass."

"Wow. That's an honest therapist."

He laughed. "She didn't say that in those exact words. She is my therapist after all. But she did show me that I've been selfish. She explained to me that the things I do in my career to help me move forward don't work so well in my personal life."

I nodded. "That makes sense, in a way. You need to be ruthless and driven to get promoted."

My brother hadn't become the financial director of a company by twiddling his thumbs.

"Pretty much. Apparently, I need to learn to turn off that part of me."

"I'm glad you're working on those things." But it still didn't really explain what he was doing here. "Did you really just come to tell me thanks?"

"Yeah. I figured, with the big news, you'd understand." He raised his eyebrows. "But, now, you look confused, like you have no idea what I'm talking about."

I shook my head. "Because I don't have any idea what you're talking about. I haven't talked to Mom for a few days."

"This wouldn't have come from Mom. I thought Sloan would have told you."

Upon hearing Sloan's name, I tensed up. News and her together did not sound promising. "I haven't talked to Sloan for a long time."

Neil frowned. "That's odd. Mom said the two of you were dating, which I'd kind of wondered about since you both showed up at Melanie's house that night together." He rubbed his nose. "It also explains why you punched me."

I wanted to laugh that my brother could joke about me hitting him, but all I could manage was a sigh. "Yeah. I haven't told Mom and Dad that we broke up."

After the two of us had left my parents' house that night, I hadn't gone back after dropping Sloan off. After hearing Ted's disappointment in me and then Sloan and I fighting, I had been in no mood to be around people. And, so far, I had avoided any talk of her when my mom asked. I didn't want to tell her how I'd failed Ted and Sloan, so I always changed the subject.

"Ah," he said with a look of understanding. "Sorry to hear that."

"Yeah. Me, too."

I didn't want to talk about it anymore. I already had to sleep every night in the bedroom and look out onto the balcony where we'd had sex. It was a good thing I had plenty to do during the day to keep my mind occupied.

Perhaps too occupied since she'd gone and served me with annulment papers.

I shook my head to clear it. "Anyway, what's your news?"

"I'm going to be a father, and you're going to be an uncle."

For a second, my brain stuttered and switched the words around. I pictured Sloan heavy with my child, and my traitorous brain—and, apparently, my dick, going by the hard-on I was getting—liked the idea of her pregnant.

It's not going to happen. You don't get to have sex with Sloan anymore, I tried to telepathically communicate to my stupid erection, but it ignored me.

It didn't help that I hadn't had sex since Hawaii. My poor cock was getting sick of my hand. I was getting sick of my hand.

Jesus. I needed to stop thinking about her.

I tried to read my brother's face, but I couldn't tell what he was thinking. "Who's the mother?" I asked.

He narrowed his eyes. "Melanie."

I held up my hands. "I'm sorry. I assumed that's who it was, but you also cheated on her and gave her an STI." I shrugged. "You could have gotten someone else pregnant."

Neil's face was red. He opened his mouth to say something but stopped himself. He took a deep breath. "You're right."

"Shit, man. I think your counseling is actually working."

"Yeah? Because, right now, all I want is to call you a fuckhead even though I know you're right."

I laughed. "Go ahead. I am a fuckhead. I should have worded that better." I cleared my throat. "Let's try this again. So, you're going to be a dad. And I assume the mother is Melanie."

Neil smiled. "Yes. And, while I did catch something, I always used protection with … the other woman. My doctor thinks I got it from oral sex."

I grimaced.

"I know," he said after seeing my face. "It's another reason I'm working on not sleeping around."

"How's that working out for you?"

"It's a lot harder than I expected. My therapist says I get a mental high off of cheating or some crap like that." He looked down at the floor. "She also says I don't put enough value into my relationships, and I always see them as temporary."

"Well, if you ever need someone to stop you from doing something stupid, you can call me. I'll tell you like it is."

Neil laughed. "I might have to do that."

It felt weird, getting into touchy-feely stuff with my brother, so I changed the subject back to what we should be talking about. "Back to you being a father. Melanie's keeping the baby?"

He smiled. A true, genuine smile. "Yeah. And can you believe that I'm excited? I'm going to be a dad."

I grinned back at him. "I'm happy for you."

"Thanks, man. Anyway, that's why I came over to tell you thanks. Because, even though Melanie and I are over as a couple, I know that I want us to get along for the baby."

What do you know? My brother was making real progress, and I was very happy for him. If only I could be happy for myself, too.

Neil studied my face. "I'm sure you and Sloan will work things out."

"Yeah, hopefully," I said because I didn't want to talk about it.

But, deep down, I knew that annulment papers meant there was nothing for us to work out.

FORTY
SLOAN

MARCH—SEVERAL MONTHS LATER

"SLOAN? SLOAN, IT'S TIME."

My body rocked as someone shook me back and forth.

"Huh? Huh?" I asked, rolling onto my back. I glanced at the clock to see that it wasn't yet three in the morning.

Melanie and her huge belly stood next to my bed. "It's time."

In a second, I went from being half-asleep to wide awake. "Holy shit." I threw back the covers. "How far apart are your contractions?"

"Six minutes."

"*Six minutes*? Why the hell didn't you wake me?"

When I'd told Mel that I would be here for her and the baby, I'd meant it. I'd practically moved into her house the last two weeks as she got closer—and then surpassed—her due date. I wanted to be here in case she needed me in the middle of the night. And she hadn't even gotten me up.

"I'm waking you now."

"But the doctor said you need to go to the hospital when they get to be five minutes apart. You're sure cutting it close."

She lifted a shoulder. "I was stuck at eight and seven minutes for about two hours."

I paused at my dresser. "Okay. I take it back. Thanks for not waking me."

Mel laughed. "I knew it." She waddled toward the door. "I'm going to go get dressed and grab my to-go things. Meet you at the door?"

"I'll meet you at your bedroom, and I'll grab your to-go things. You're already carrying the fricking baby, for God's sake."

She shook her head and laughed as she walked out of the room.

I hurriedly got dressed, combed my hair, and grabbed my keys and purse in record time, only to find Mel's bedroom empty.

I stomped to the front door. "Melanie."

"What?" she called from the kitchen.

"You're eating?" I asked when I entered.

"Yeah."

"Shouldn't we be going to the hospital?"

"It's not five minutes yet."

"Let's go anyway."

She shook her head. "Nah."

"Melanie Carlson," I said, using my firm voice.

She rolled her eyes. "Fine. We'll go."

It was no wonder half the people at the OB clinic thought Melanie and I were a couple. We kind of acted like one.

While Neil had been making a real effort to be involved, he couldn't always get off work. Since my schedule was flexible, I often went with her. Speaking of the baby daddy ...

"Have you called Neil yet?"

Melanie bent over and clutched the wall as a contraction started.

I looked at my watch so that I could count the time in between this and the next one.

When her pain eased, Mel stood. "No, I was going to call him when we got in the car."

"Okay then, let's go and do this thing."

———

I might have been ready, and Melanie might have been ready, but Baby Carlson was not ready. She or he refused to come out.

"There's still time, Melanie, but if the baby's heart rate drops any lower, we're going to have to do a C-section."

Neil and I exchanged looks across Mel's bed. She didn't have much of a birth plan, except that she didn't want a C-section. However, it was almost five o'clock the following evening. She'd been in labor for over thirty-six hours, so maybe she'd be happy to get the baby out.

"Noooooo," Melanie whined. "Come out, baby."

Or maybe not.

The doctor chuckled. "I think the little one is trying to show you who the new boss is," she said. She put her hand on Melanie's knee. "I know you're scared, but I have performed hundreds of C-sections, and the best way to lower your risk is to go in before it's an emergency."

Mel looked heartbroken, but she nodded.

The doctor smiled reassuringly. "We're not there yet, so relax for now, okay?"

Melanie nodded.

The doctor went to the door and turned. "Oh, and I hate to give you more bad news, but if we do go into surgery, only one person is allowed to come." She looked at Neil and me. "I'm sorry, guys."

I smiled. Worrying about us should be the last thing the doctor thought about.

After the doctor left, I turned to Melanie and Neil. "If you go to surgery, I think Neil should go in the room."

Melanie grabbed my hand. "But I want you." She stuck out her bottom lip.

Apparently, birth turned my friend into a child again.

I squeezed her hand. "I want that, too, but think about your baby. How would she or he feel if she or he found out that you wouldn't let her or his father into the room to see her or him delivered?" I made a frustrated noise. "You know, this pep talk would sound a lot better if I didn't have to keep using all the pronouns. Why didn't you find out what you're having again?"

Melanie crossed her arms over her chest. "Because I didn't wanna."

I looked at Neil. "She's all yours."

He smiled at me and pulled up a chair next to Melanie's bed. "If you really want Sloan to go in there, we'll figure out what to tell the baby someday."

I had to give Neil props. He'd come a long way. If he had been this nice to Mel when they were dating, she might not have broken up with him. That, and the cheating, of course. But then again, if things had gone differently, my friend might not be having a baby today.

Melanie slammed her fists down on the bed. "But I want both of you to go in there."

I squeezed her shoulder. "Let's not worry about it until we have to, okay?"

As the next hour wore on, it was apparent that Melanie's labor wasn't progressing, and she would have to go to surgery. I convinced her that having Neil go into surgery was the best thing for everyone. And, while I was sad that I wouldn't get to be in the room when the baby was born, Neil was the father, and it was the right call.

With the room now empty, all the excitement wheeled to another room, I was beat. I had managed to go to Mel's house since she lived closer and sneak in a shower that morning, but I hadn't gotten much sleep since Mel woke me up in the middle of the night. I'd camped out in her room last night, but it had been a lot of broken sleep.

I stole one of her blankets off the pile on the counter and lay down on the couch in Melanie's hospital room. If I could get in even a half hour, I'd feel a lot better.

FORTY-ONE

CALEB

I GOT off the elevator and looked at the room number signs before heading right.

My brother had called and asked me to bring some food, as he had been at the hospital all day and was starving. Last I had heard, they were taking Melanie into surgery.

Any minute now, I was going to be an uncle. I was surprised at how excited I was about my new nephew or niece, but over the last six months, I'd grown closer to Neil. We were never going to be great friends, but we did try to hang out a couple of times a month at least.

When I reached the doorway of Melanie's room, the bed was gone, and there was a long figure curled up on the couch.

It was Sloan.

I entered the room and quietly set the food down on the counter before approaching her.

She looked very peaceful in her sleep, and I had to resist the urge to touch her. I knew she deserved her rest after hearing that Melanie had been in labor for a day and a half.

But, man, did I miss her. I missed touching her and talking to her.

It was probably a good thing she was sleeping, or I'd probably make a fool of myself.

Just as I was about to turn and head to the chair, Sloan stirred and rolled onto her back.

She smiled up at me as she yawned and stretched.

I grinned down at her.

"Hey, husband," she said in a low voice.

"Hey, wife."

DECEMBER

"Caleb, can you come back here?"

I said good-bye to the customer I'd just rung up and turned to the rear of the store.

Ted wanted to talk to me.

"Sure." I did a quick sweep to make sure the store wasn't too busy and then headed back to Ted's office.

"Have a seat," he said when I entered.

I had no idea what this was about. I'd been the model employee since Ted found out about my lying. I'd even come in when I was sick a month ago to show how loyal I was to the store.

It had kind of backfired because everyone had stood three feet away from me, and Ted had made me go home.

"What's going on?" I asked after pulling up the chair.

"I have some news."

Ted's face was grim, and I didn't have a good feeling.

"Okay." I told myself, no matter what it was, I wasn't going to get upset.

"I've changed my mind about selling the store. I'd like to have everything finalized before spring. Mary wants us to start traveling after the snow melts."

I took a deep breath and blew it out. "That's … great. I'm happy for you. You both deserve it." I stood. "And thank you for telling me in private." It would have been hard to hear from someone else that Rick was buying the store.

"Caleb, sit down."

I really didn't want to, but I owed it to Ted.

"You don't understand," he said once I was in my seat again.

"You're right. I don't," I said because, at this point, I had no idea what he was talking about.

"I'm going to sell the store to Rick."

I looked down. Ted was wrong. I understood completely.

"And to you."

I swung my head up. "What?"

"I've decided to sell the store to both of you. Fifty-fifty split. You will be partners. I've already okayed it with Rick. Now, I need to know if you're on board."

Wow. Ted was going to sell me his store. Sure, it was only half of it, but it was more than I could dream about at this point.

I should be ecstatic. It was what I had wanted for months and months, but it suddenly felt like a hollow victory. Sure, I felt great that Ted was no longer mad at me, and he trusted me enough to hand over his pride and joy to me. Half of his pride and joy.

But it didn't mean as much to me when I felt like there was something missing in my life. Inside me.

I still missed Sloan like crazy.

I had thought my feelings for her would have faded by now, but I couldn't stop thinking about her.

My brother, of all people, had told me I was in love with her. When he first said it, I laughed in his face. But, later that night, as I'd lain in bed, I'd realized he might be right.

I'd had girlfriends in the past. Some serious. Some not serious. I never told any of them I loved them, and now, I knew why. I'd been sad when some of those relationships ended, but the women had quickly become an afterthought. Not one of them occupied my mind months later.

"What's wrong, Caleb? I thought you'd be happy. You know this is the best I can do with what happened," Ted said, sounding concerned.

I thought about keeping my feelings to myself, but I had promised no more lying. "I know, and I understand. I am happy. It's just … I miss … Sloan. She's the first person I thought of, and I would love to tell her the good news."

After going to Ted's house and getting yelled at by him, I hadn't brought up Sloan's name once. I'd been too afraid.

"You still care about her?" Ted asked with what sounded like displeasure.

"Yes," I admitted. And, since I had gone that far, I decided to tell Ted everything. "I blackmailed Sloan into being my girlfriend."

Ted's eyebrows shot up, practically to his hairline.

"I didn't even know her that well, but she was there, and you had told me to bring my girlfriend to dinner, so I blackmailed her." I met Ted's eyes. "She's not a bad person, and I hate that you think she is. Also"—I cleared my throat—"we actually grew to care for each other."

I laughed at the memory of Hawaii.

"You're probably going to think this is nuts, but the two of us really got married. We'd had a bit too much to drink, but our little impromptu ceremony was never about deceiving you. That was all Sloan and me."

Ted smiled. "I knew you really got married."

I frowned. "You did?"

"Yes. Sloan told Mary."

"Oh." I wondered when she had done that.

"And I've been watching you the last few months. You're not the same, Caleb."

"I've been working very hard to prove myself to you."

"To prove yourself to me or to forget about Sloan?"

I shrugged. "I don't know. Maybe both."

Ted smiled reassuringly. "Well, I want you to know that I harbor no hard feelings toward her, and I apologize for rushing to judgment. But, if you broke up with her for me, I really wish you hadn't."

I shook my head. "No. We got into a big fight and broke things off. I didn't see her again for a month, and I apologized and let her know I wasn't mad anymore. Her response was to send me annulment papers."

"Ooh." Ted winced.

"Yeah."

"Have you talked to her at all? Have you tried to work it out?"

I shook my head again. "I put the ball in her court."

Ted laughed, and I had a feeling it was at me.

I frowned. "I don't understand what's so funny."

"Boy, you should be on your knees in front of that girl every day, begging for her to take you back."

"What?"

"After everything you put her through? And you thought a, *Hey, I'm sorry we fought*, would bring her around?" Ted laughed some more.

Meanwhile, I was beginning to feel like a jackass.

I crossed my arms over my chest. "Yeah, well, it's too late now."

It took a couple more seconds for Ted to stop laughing, but when he did, he asked, "Did you sign those annulment papers?"

My face turned red because I'd thrown them in a stack of other papers and forgotten about them. I thought I had forgotten on purpose. "Um … no."

Ted lifted his brow. "Has she bugged you about signing them? Has her lawyer contacted you?"

I thought about it, and it was like someone had turned on a lightbulb in my head. "No."

"Then, I think there's still a chance."

"Really?"

Ted shrugged. "There's only one way to find out."

I jumped out of my chair. "I have to go."

Ted smiled. "I figured as much." He nodded toward the door. "Get out of here."

I stood in front of Sloan's door, praying she was home.

When I heard Bear bark and Sloan telling him to hush, it was music to my ears.

And, when she opened the door, seeing her standing there was the most beautiful sight I'd ever seen.

"Caleb?" she said, surprised. "What are you doing here?"

I pulled the annulment papers from my jacket and held them in front of her. "I don't want to sign these," I said and ripped them in half.

Sloan raised her brow and said, "You know I can just call and get a new set sent out."

I stepped forward until I felt the warmth of her house and the warmth of her body near mine. "Then, I'll just rip them up, too."

She tilted her head to the side. "Why?"

The fact that she wasn't mad gave me hope.

"Because I've realized something."

"Oh? And what's that?"

"You promised me five dates. You still owe me one."

FORTY-TWO
SLOAN

MARCH

I SAT up and pulled Caleb down next to me on the couch in the hospital room. I wrapped my arms around his neck and kissed him. "I've missed you."

He pushed my hair back from my face. "I've missed you, too. I prayed every night that Mel's baby would come, so you'd be able to come home." He kissed me again. "Our bed is lonely without you." He kissed my neck. "My penis is lonely without you."

I laughed loudly at this. "I came home for a quickie two days ago."

He continued to kiss my neck and shoulder. "I know. But I need more than five minutes with you."

"Why? We already don't know what to do with the other four and a half."

Caleb lifted his head and scowled. "You're not funny."

I grinned. "I'm hilarious." I looked over at the counter and saw a fast-food bag. "Ooh, is that food?"

"Yes, but you can't have any now that you've made fun of my manhood."

I laid my head on his chest and batted my eyelashes at him. "Oh, Caleb, you are the stallion of lovers. You are the king of orgasms. You are—"

"If I tell you that I brought you your favorite thing to eat, will you stop?"

I lifted my head. "Yes."

"Go on. It's in the bag."

I scrambled off the couch to get the food. I hadn't realized how hungry I was until I saw the bag. I quickly pulled everything out.

"The rest is for Neil," Caleb explained when I gave him a questioning look about the food. "It was his request."

I stuck a delicious fry in my mouth, and Caleb grinned.

I couldn't help but smile back. And, to think, we could have practically been strangers again at the birth of Mel's baby if he hadn't shown up at my house back in December.

DECEMBER

I stared at Caleb and the two halves of paper in his hands, not sure what to think of him showing up on my doorstep months later, demanding I owe him another date.

I had spent the whole day showing homes to my cousin, Cal, who was moving back to Minnesota, and I was exhausted. He was only in town for two days before he had to go back to New York where he currently lived. Not only did I cram a lot showings into one day, but every time I said his name, it reminded me of Caleb, making my heart hurt.

And now Caleb was here.

Bear knocked me out of the way to get to him, and one foot touched the cold cement outside.

"Hey, buddy," Caleb said to my dog, who had no qualms about letting Caleb know he had missed him.

I sighed. "You might as well come in. It's cold out, and I don't feel like freezing."

Caleb ushered Bear inside, and I closed the door.

"You changed everything around," Caleb said.

After we'd broken up, I'd needed a change, so I'd rearranged my furniture. It was a nice change, and all it had cost me was some labor.

"Yeah," I said, not wanting to tell him why. I crossed my arms over my chest. "Why are you really here?"

He spun around. "I told you, I want our last date."

"What's the point?"

A flash of hurt crossed Caleb's face, but it disappeared as fast as it'd appeared. "I want a second chance."

I sighed and stepped forward to take the stupid annulment papers out of his hands. If I was honest, I had hoped that filing for an annulment would spur Caleb to take some action. But that had been almost two months ago. Now, I simply felt tired.

I went to the kitchen with Caleb following me, and I threw the papers in the garbage before turning back around.

"Caleb, you don't need a second chance. You didn't mess up. We got in a fight and broke up."

If he knew what some of my exes had done, he'd give himself an award for Best Boyfriend of the Year.

Although had he ever really been my boyfriend? We'd kind of gone from a weird arrangement to screwing to getting married. No wonder we'd broken up.

"Yes, I did."

"Yes, you did what?" I'd been thinking so hard that I'd lost our conversation.

"I screwed up," he said.

I smiled and thought, *Fuck it.*

"Screwing up is cheating on someone; screwing up is stealing money from your girlfriend's purse; screwing up is moving away when your girlfriend is gone for the weekend and not telling her."

Caleb's eyes were wide with shock. "Did all these things happen to you?"

I lifted a shoulder. "Maybe."

He shook his head. "Wow. Those guys were real assholes."

I snorted. "Tell me something I don't already know."

He stepped forward. "Give me another chance. I'm not like those guys."

I actually did already know that, which probably made our breakup feel even worse. With all the others, I had been furious and wanted nothing more to do with them. With Caleb, I still thought about him every day.

He pushed my hair behind my ear and ran his thumb down my cheek. "God, I've missed you."

I didn't want to admit that I felt the same about him, so I kissed him instead.

I had only intended it to be a sweet kiss, but Caleb opened his mouth and licked the seam of my lips. I automatically opened for him, and the taste of him on my tongue had me groaning.

I hadn't had sex since Hawaii, and I was horny.

I briefly wondered if Caleb had slept with anyone since then, but I quickly blocked out that thought. I didn't want anything to deflate my lady boner.

Caleb picked me up and set me on the counter. Pulling my ass toward him, he shoved his erection between my legs.

I reached between our bodies and cupped him. I'd missed his dick almost as much as I'd missed the rest of him.

I tore my mouth from his and went for the button of his jeans. I was ready to hop off the counter and get on my knees, but Caleb put a hand on mine to stop me.

"What are you doing?"

He shook his head. "No."

"Are you kidding me? I am willing to have sex with you, no strings attached, and you don't want to?"

He chuckled. "I never said I didn't want to. I haven't had sex since the last time with you in Hawaii. I'm dying to be inside you."

I grinned and tried to go for his button again. "Let's do this then."

He squeezed my wrist. "No."

I looked into his face. "You are sending the most awful mixed signals right now."

He dropped his head against mine and groaned. "I'm sorry. It's just that I know I'll fall into bed with you, and I'll forget all about getting an answer to my question."

"What question?"

"See? You've already forgotten."

I shook my head. I still didn't remember.

"I want one more date. Will you give me one?"

I really didn't want to go through the process of getting back together and calling it quits again, but I wanted to get laid, damn it. "Fine. I'll give you one last date. Now, take off your pants."

He grinned and brought my hands to my chest. He tenderly kissed me and stepped back.

"New Year's Eve," he said.

"What?"

"New Year's Eve. That's the date I want."

"That's over three weeks away."

"I know. But I need time."

I threw up my hands. "Fine. New Year's it is. Now, get back over here."

Taking a step back, he shook his head. "No sex until our date."

"Are you kidding me?"

He had to be joking.

He shook his head again. "No. I want to do this right. We have to wait." He turned around and headed for my door. "Bye, Bear," he said, patting my dog on the head. He opened my door and turned. "I'll see you on the thirty-first."

"I hate you," I said.

He grinned. "No, you don't." He stepped outside and shut the door.

He was right. I didn't hate him at all. Instead, I was ridiculously in love with him.

Bear lifted his head and looked at me.

"Shut up. You didn't tell him you loved him either."

FORTY-THREE
CALEB

NEW YEAR'S EVE

I LOOKED around my house to make sure everything was perfect and patted my pocket to make sure my surprise was there. I kept worrying it was going to fall out.

My house was crammed with people, yet part of me felt like I was all alone. I knew it was the nerves, but it still made me want to puke.

Melanie walked up to me. "You ready? Sloan should be here any minute."

I took a deep breath. "As ready as I'll ever be."

She squeezed my forearm. "You're going to be fine. Everything will work out."

"I hope you're right. Thanks for all your help."

When I had called Melanie to tell her I needed her help with getting Sloan back, she'd jumped at the chance. I'd thought she'd tell me to go screw myself, but she'd told me that she'd secretly been rooting for Sloan and me to be together for a long time.

She smiled. "No problem. But, if things go to hell for some reason, I had nothing to do with this."

I frowned. "You just said everything would work out."

"Because that's what people do when someone is nervous."

"Gee, thanks."

She slapped me on the shoulder. "You're welcome," she said as she walked away.

"That was sarcasm," I called to her, but Melanie didn't turn back around.

She ran into Sloan's parents and started talking to them.

My brother came up to me next. "You look like you're going to hurl."

"Thanks," I said dryly.

"You're welcome."

"What is it with everyone not getting my sarcasm tonight?"

"Oh. Uh … I guess you're not welcome then." Neil clearly didn't know how to make me feel better.

I shook my head. "I know I probably look bad, but I can't help it."

"Sorry, man. Maybe you'll get lucky, and she won't show."

I narrowed my eyes. "Now, why would you go and say something like that?"

He shrugged. "Hey. I'm trying to help."

"Yeah, well, try harder."

Neil opened his mouth just as the doorbell rang.

The house went from a dozen conversations going on at once to complete silence.

"Keep talking, everyone," I said. "I don't want her to feel like she's on display."

The doorbell rang. I took a deep breath, and I opened the door.

Sloan stood on the other side, looking beautiful. Under her open coat, she wore a black dress that made her red hair stand out.

"Hey," I greeted her.

"Hi." She looked around me. "I didn't know it was going to be a party."

I stepped off to the side. "Come in before you freeze to death."

"Thank you," she said.

"Let me take your coat."

She smiled. "Wow. What a gentleman."

"I try." Not really. "At least, tonight, I do," I amended. "It's a special occasion." And I didn't just mean the holiday.

After hanging Sloan's jacket in the front closet, Ted and Mary approached us, and she took a step back toward me.

I put my hand on her lower back to show her that I supported her.

Mary smiled first. "Hello, Sloan."

"Hi, Mary."

"Sloan," Ted said with a nod. "It's good to see you again."

Sloan looked over her shoulder at me.

I smiled. "It's okay. We worked it all out. I told them everything."

Her eyes grew wide. "Really?" she whispered.

I laughed. "Really."

"Caleb's right. And I apologize for anything I said," Ted said.

"You were upset," Sloan responded. "I can see why you didn't want me around."

Ted winced. "Caleb told you I'd said that, huh?"

"I might have been eavesdropping," she admitted, only looking the slightest bit guilty.

I laughed.

"Can we call it even?" Ted asked. "You're good for Caleb, and I don't want any hard feelings between us."

"Let's forget it ever happened," Sloan said.

Ted pointed a finger at her. "Not too much forgetting now, or you and Caleb wouldn't be together."

Sloan looked at me, and I shrugged.

"I tried telling him it was only a date tonight, but he's already convinced that you and I are a thing again."

Sloan turned back to Ted. "I guess you're right about that. It did bring Caleb and me together."

I squeezed her waist. I took her comment as a good sign.

Mary opened her arms. "Give me a hug, dear."

Sloan laughed and let Mary engulf her.

They pulled apart, and Mary said, "I agree with Ted. I'm so happy Caleb found you. He's going to need your help with the store."

Sloan's head swung around once again to look at me, and I shrugged sheepishly.

"Ted's letting me buy half of it."

She turned toward me and flung her arms around my neck. "Caleb, that's the best news."

"It is," I said, holding her tight.

I didn't want to let her go; she felt incredible in my arms.

But my lower anatomy had started paying attention, and if I didn't want to walk around with a hard-on in front of everyone, I had better let her go.

"Come," I said. "I want to show you who else is here."

I brought her over to my friends.

"Sloan, this is Blake and Griffin."

She shook their hands. "It's nice to know Caleb has friends. I was beginning to think he was a loser."

Griffin and Blake laughed. I tried not to since I was the butt of her joke, but I thought it was a good thing that she was making fun of me.

"I think that's enough of the three of you getting to know each other," I said. "Let's move on."

"I like them," Sloan said as we walked away. "They laugh at my jokes."

"Yeah, you're a real riot."

It was her turn to laugh. "You're so cute when you get upset."

I grinned. She'd called me cute. Another good sign.

Sloan was surprised to see Melanie, and that was also when she began to wonder if the party was for more than just a party. I evaded her questions the few times she'd asked though because I wasn't ready to tell her.

When she saw that her parents were at my house, she gave me several questioning looks.

"You invited my parents?" she said to me. "How?"

"Melanie called us, honey," her mom, Bonnie, said.

"We were more than happy to come," her father, Chad, added. "But can you explain to me why I had to hear it from some guy—no offense, Caleb—who I'd never met that you'd gotten married?"

Sloan's face turned red to match her hair, and she shot daggers at me.

I shrugged. "They're your parents. They needed to know."

She put her hands on her hips. "Oh? And do your parents know?"

I pointed in the direction of the kitchen. "They do now. They're in there."

"Oh." Some of the fire left her. "Well, now, I don't know what to say because I was expecting a different answer from you."

I laughed.

Sloan's mom put her hand on Sloan's arm. "You and I are having lunch next week. I want to hear all about you and Caleb."

Sloan nodded as her parents walked away.

She turned to me. "Okay, Caleb, this is more than some date. What is going on?"

FORTY-FOUR
SLOAN

CALEB PICKED up a glass of champagne from the kitchen, got up on a chair, and clinked a butter knife against the drink. "Can I have your attention, please?"

Everyone quieted down, and he turned to me.

"In case you don't know the full story, I'm going to give you the CliffsNotes version," he said to the group. "Sloan and I've known each other for a while. Her best friend dated my brother. But we didn't know each other very well at that time."

Caleb looked around the room.

"All that changed when I convinced Sloan to help me out with a little problem I was having at work. See, my boss" —Ted raised his hand and waved—"thought I was a flight risk when I asked him if I could buy his store. So, I might have lied to him and told him I had a girlfriend."

Caleb's audience chuckled.

"What I hadn't planned on was the need to find a flesh-and-blood woman to be said girlfriend." He held his hand out to me. "This is where Sloan came in. I had to convince

—and when I say convince, I mean, *convince*—her to play my girlfriend. She did so—reluctantly." He tapped his chin. "I believe she told me she was going to call me *Loser* in her phone, if that gives you any indication of how she felt about me."

I blushed as everyone laughed around us.

"But she did agree, loser or no loser, and our agreement was for five dates." Caleb's face turned from joking to sentimental. "Everything was going pretty well for these dates … until my boss invited us to go to Hawaii."

Everyone oohed.

"I know, right? Anyway, Sloan classified Hawaii as our fourth date. But, by this time, ladies and gentlemen, we'd been hanging out quite some time. Well, one thing led to another, and with the help of some alcohol, Sloan and I tied the knot in Hawaii."

Murmurs went around the room, and I wanted to hide. He was telling everyone what had happened between us with only a few details omitted or changed to make the situation sound better. I didn't want people to know he'd blackmailed me either, so I liked how he'd used the word *convince*.

"But, folks, that's not the end of the story," Caleb continued. "You see, my boss and my father ran into each other, and the secret came out once we got back home. It wasn't a good start to a marriage, and Sloan and I went our separate ways."

"Ahh," everyone around us said in disappointment.

Caleb put his hand to his heart. "I know. I know." He held up a finger. "But I suddenly remembered that Sloan owed me another date."

"Are you still married?" someone yelled from the back of

the room.

"Hold on, I'll get to that," Caleb answered. "You see, Sloan thought I didn't care about her anymore and sent me annulment papers. But I convinced her to come out tonight, using our fifth and last date as leverage. And, now, you're probably wondering what all of you are doing here."

I nodded along with everyone else.

Caleb smiled at me. "I wanted to come clean with everyone, and I wanted Sloan to know that there is nothing left to hide. There isn't anything that people don't know now." He looked at me and stepped off the chair. "Because, if we're going to make this marriage work, then we need a fresh start. No secrets. Just you and me, together," he said.

Tears sprang to my eyes.

He handed me his champagne. "Hold this for me, please."

I didn't even question it. I just took it from him. But, when he got down on one knee, I wanted to pound the whole thing. Unfortunately, I was frozen in my spot.

Caleb pulled out my engagement/wedding ring from his pocket. "Mel snuck it from your house for me."

My eyes beelined for my friend. She shrugged and grinned.

"Sloan?"

I looked down at Caleb.

"Will you do me the honor of giving our marriage a chance and being my wife? If it doesn't work out, I will sign your annulment papers without a fight."

The room was so silent; I could hear the ticking of the clock on the wall.

It was hard to say no to that, except one glaring thing

seemed to be missing in this scenario. And, while I didn't want to embarrass him, I had to ask, "Why?"

He stood and grinned. "Because I love you, of course."

I burst into tears and threw my arms around his neck, almost knocking him over and spilling his champagne.

Caleb chuckled in my ear. "Does this mean yes?"

"I love you, too," I said. I took a step back, so everyone could hear me. "Yes."

The room erupted in applause and hoots and hollers.

Caleb stood and pulled another ring from his pocket. It was a man's ring, and he handed it to me right before he slipped my ring back on my left finger.

I looked down at his ring. It was silver in color like mine, and in the middle were three tiny stones. A diamond and our two birthstones.

My breath caught, and I looked at him.

He smiled. "I needed three weeks to get the ring made," he explained. "I wanted you to know I meant what I said." He held up his left hand. "Will you do the honors?"

I nodded and pushed the ring onto his finger.

"It's midnight," someone yelled, and the room cheered.

Caleb smiled. "To new beginnings and a new year?"

I nodded and grinned back. "To new beginnings." I held up the single crystal in my hand. "We can't even clink glasses and cheers."

He put his hand over mine. "Then, we'll share. Just like we're going to do for the rest of our lives."

He took a sip and put the glass to my lips for me to do the same.

"You're pretty sure of yourself," I teased.

He shook his head. "Wrong. I'm pretty sure about *you*."

FORTY-FIVE

CALEB

MARCH

"LOOK AT HER," Sloan said, picking up one of the baby's fingers. "She's so little."

I put my arm around my wife and looked at Neil and Melanie. "What did you decide to name her?"

"Yeah," Sloan chimed in. "I've been dying to know what name you picked out." She stuck out her bottom lip. "I still can't believe you wouldn't tell your best friend."

Melanie laughed. "I was in labor for a day and a half, I just had my belly cut open, and the doctor pulled a human being out of me. I do not feel sorry for you."

"Burn," Sloan said.

Everyone chuckled.

"But the name we picked out is …" Melanie looked at Neil for confirmation. "Carly Marie Stanton. Carly is for Carlson. Marie is because it has an *I* and *E* in it, like both our names," she said, gesturing between herself and Neil. "And because I'm a dork."

"I like it," Sloan said.

"And, after much debate, we decided on Stanton because I hope to get married someday. I want Carly to have the last name of one of her parents."

"You could always just not change your last name when you get hitched," Sloan offered.

"Okay, *Sloan Stanton*. I'll take that into consideration."

"Hey. I thought about not changing my last name."

"It's true," I said. I wouldn't say I'd worked hard to convince her to take my last name, but I had offered her several orgasms in return.

"He bribed me," Sloan said.

"Hey," I protested. "The joke's on you because I would have given you what you wanted even if you had said no."

Sloan grinned at me and wiggled her brow. "I know."

"Are you two talking about sex?" Melanie asked.

Neither of us answered. I was too busy thinking about how much I loved having sex with my wife.

"They're talking about sex," Melanie said, answering her own question. "If you two don't stop making *fuck me* eyes at each other, I'm taking my baby back."

That got Sloan's attention. "Sorry," she said to her friend.

"No, you're not. But I forgive you."

A nurse walked into the room, knocking on the door as she entered. She smiled politely. "It's getting late, and Mom has some rest she needs to catch up on."

I looked at the clock on the wall. "I suppose visiting hours are over."

The nurse nodded. "Technically, yes. Dad, you're more

than welcome to stay. And, normally, I wouldn't ask you to leave, but my patient needs her rest."

"Say no more," Sloan said. She kissed baby Carly on the head. "I'll see you tomorrow. By the way, I'm your aunt Sloan. Don't forget it." She put the baby back in Melanie's arms.

"I'm sure she's writing it down as we speak," I said.

Sloan stood straight and smacked me in the chest.

"*Hey.*"

"Quit making fun of me."

"Said the woman who told me I lasted thirty seconds."

Everyone gave me a funny look.

I shook my head. "Never mind." I leaned closer and whispered, "But, for the record, I last a lot longer than that. *A lot* longer."

Sloan rolled her eyes and pulled on my arm. "They don't care, Caleb."

"I care," I said as I followed her out of the room. Once we were in the hall, I put my arm around her and pulled her close. "I can't let you or anyone else think I don't satisfy you."

She kissed my cheek. "You know you do. But ..."

Uh-oh. That didn't sound good.

"But what?"

"I kind of want one now."

I was clueless. "Want what?"

"A baby."

I stopped walking. "Are you serious?"

"Yeah. I suppose this is one of those things we should have talked about before marriage."

That line was a running joke between the two of us. Usually, it was little things, like how we loaded the dishwasher or where to keep the extra sheets. This was a lot bigger than how we cleaned the dishes or where we stored stuff in the house.

"Please tell me you want kids someday." Sloan looked nervous now.

There was an open patient room right next to us, and I pulled her inside. I pushed the door closed and kissed her.

Sloan momentarily went with me, fisting her hands in my shirt and then running her fingers down over my abdomen and slipping the tips into the waistband of my jeans.

I thrust my hips toward her, so she could feel how hard I was.

I broke my mouth from hers to kiss down her neck.

"Does this mean, yes, you want kids? Or are you trying to distract me because you don't want to tell me no?"

I pulled back from her to meet her eyes. "The second I heard that Mel was pregnant, I pictured you pregnant instead."

"And how did that make you feel?"

"I beat off to the image for at least a week."

Sloan kissed me. "That should be wrong, but it's so hot to hear you say that."

I yanked her to me and picked her up. "What do you say we get started right now?" I asked as I carried her over to the bed.

She laughed. "I'm on the pill."

"Then, get off of it."

"It'll still take time."

"I'll settle for a practice round then."

I laid Sloan on the bed, pulled off her pants, yanked mine off my hips, and pushed inside her.

EPILOGUE

SLOAN

SEVERAL YEARS LATER

"CALEB," I called. "You need to hurry up," I yelled up the stairs. "Everyone is going to be here soon, and I need some help with the boys."

My handsome husband bound down the stairs a couple of minutes later. "What do you need, baby?"

"Colton's in the high chair. Grayson's in the pack-and-play, and Carter is running around, naked." I sighed. "And I still have to get the rest of dinner finished."

Caleb turned around but quickly spun back to me. "What do you want me to do first?"

Carter, our oldest at four, had a new thing of taking his clothes off and running around without them until I or his father caught him. Tonight, I didn't have time to chase after him.

Grayson was our two-year-old and wanted to do everything his brother did. He was way past big enough to be free of the pack-and-play, but if I let him go, he'd take off his clothes, too, and then we'd end up with pee on the floor. He was still potty-training.

Colton was the baby at nine months. I hadn't known what else to do with him, so I stuck him in the high chair with some stuff he could snack on.

"Find Carter. He needs to get dressed before Carly gets here and points out to everyone that he has a penis."

Caleb nodded. "Right. Carter. No penis-pointing. Clothes."

Ten minutes later, Caleb came back with a giggling Carter over his shoulders. Caleb set him down and got his serious face out. "You will leave your clothes on or no dessert."

"Okay, Daddy."

Caleb ruffled his hair. "Go play."

Carter ran off.

"What's next?" he asked, coming behind me and slipping his arms around my waist. "I have a really good idea."

I laughed and shook him off. I turned and gave him a kiss. "Your brother and Helen will be here soon. He's always so annoyingly early."

"Five minutes is early?"

"It is for dinner."

Caleb shrugged. "Okay."

"Can you change Grayson's diaper and put some pants on him?"

"What's with all our kids being naked?"

"They're not all naked."

Colton giggled, and we looked over at the baby.

I'd forgotten that he was only wearing a bib and a diaper. I threw a hand up. "Fine. They're all naked." I poked Caleb in the chest. "It's because you had to give me all boys. I wanted one girl. One."

Caleb grabbed an olive from the veggie tray beside me. "Sorry, babe. I had a long talk with the boys, but they didn't listen to me."

"The boys? Are you talking about your testicles?"

He wrinkled his nose. "They're called balls, babe. Or nuts."

I rolled my eyes. "Whatever they're called, they failed you."

He scoffed. "Hardly. They gave me three sons. Soon, we'll have a football team."

"In your dreams." I circled the area in front of my uterus. "This shop is closed."

Caleb wiggled his eyebrows. "But I have the key."

I snorted. "I changed the locks."

Caleb laughed as the doorbell rang.

I looked at the clock. It was fifteen minutes to six. "See? I told you. He's early."

Caleb shrugged. "It's fine. My brother can help me. It's not like he doesn't have a kid with another on the way."

"Run along then. I need to finish cooking."

Caleb went to the living room. I heard him say a few words to Grayson before he answered the door. The sound of Neil's and Helen's voices filled the other room a few seconds later.

I was proud of how far Neil had come. He was a great father to Carly, and he treated his wife, Helen, great. I would just like it if he showed up fifteen minutes later, like everyone else.

As if my friend could read my mind, Melanie and her

husband, Jon, showed up with Carly twenty minutes later. I was just taking dinner off the stove and turning off the oven when they arrived.

I walked into the living room with a smile on my face and put my arm around my husband. I looked up into his face and grinned.

"What's got you so happy?" he said.

"You."

"Yeah?"

"Yeah. Thanks for convincing me to go on our last date."

He kissed the side of my head. "The pleasure is all mine."

MY WRONG NUMBER SAMPLE

INDY

"Listen, Indy, you need to just call him up, tell him to get his ass over to your house, and demand that he fuck you."

I sighed and popped a French fry in my mouth. My best friend had my best interests at heart, but things with Joel hadn't progressed to the sex stage yet.

Not because I hadn't wanted it to, but because he hadn't. At least, that was how it felt. I'd put out the signals, but he wasn't picking them up.

"I don't think that will work," I told Leslie. "We haven't even exchanged phone numbers yet."

We were having our usual after-work dinner and drinks on Friday night, and this wasn't the first time Leslie had brought up my sex life. I usually changed the subject and brushed her off, but tonight was different. I was tired of waiting for Joel to make a move and wanted her opinion.

Leslie set her beer down with such force that I was

worried alcohol would spill onto her hand, her blue eyes full of surprise. "Indy, you haven't even exchanged phone numbers?" she asked incredulously, pushing her strawberry-blonde hair over her shoulder. "You've gone on two dates. How do you communicate? And how did I not know this?"

"Three dates," I corrected. "And we always message each other through the dating app. You know that I don't give out my number right away for safety reasons."

"Serial killer."

"What?" I was confused.

"You either think he's a serial killer or he thinks you're a serial killer. That's why you haven't swapped numbers."

"I am not a serial killer."

Leslie put a finger to her chest. "*I* know you're not a serial killer. But does Joel know that?"

"Of course."

She picked up a fry and pointed it at me. "But you didn't say he wasn't a killer. Maybe you secretly think he'll murder you in your sleep."

I shook my head. "You need to stop listening to so many true-crime podcasts."

"Never. But seriously, do you have any subconscious reservations about him?"

I dug deep and really thought about the question before answering, "Well …"

"Well what?" Leslie probed.

"I don't think he's a bad guy, but I do worry he might be too much of a good guy."

She smiled knowingly and pointed at me. "You think he's going to be a dud in bed."

"The thought has occurred to me."

"Personally, bad sex is still sex. And you, my friend, need to get laid. You've been crabby. How long has it been?"

"Too long."

"How long?"

I sighed. "About sixteen months."

"No wonder you're such a bitch."

I picked up a fry and threw it at her. "Just because you get some on the regular doesn't mean you can call me names."

Leslie laughed. "Okay, how about bitchy? My sweet, mild-mannered friend has been bitchy for the last few months."

I rolled my eyes. "You wouldn't be completely wrong. I have been on edge recently. But I don't agree about the bad-sex thing. Nothing's worse than having to sneak off to the bathroom to get yourself off after doing the deed because he got his and I didn't."

Leslie made a disgusted face. "Have I ever told you how much I dislike your ex?"

"Constantly," I said dryly.

"Good. I just wanted to make sure you knew to never get back together with him."

"He's already got a new girlfriend. You have nothing to worry about."

Leslie took a drink of her beer. "So, Mr. Bad Sex is getting some, and you're not. Criminal, Indy. That is criminal."

I shrugged. "So, what do I do?"

The server chose that moment to show up.

"You're young and good-looking," Leslie said to him.

"Uh … thanks."

"Don't worry. I'm not hitting on you. I need a man's perspective on this."

The guy relaxed. "Shoot."

"My friend here met this guy on a dating app. They've gone on three dates, but neither of them has gone home with the other. Don't you think that's weird? My friend needs to get laid. Do you think the guy is putting her off? What should she do?"

The server whistled while I covered my eyes.

"Thanks for laying it all out there like that, Leslie."

She held up her hands. "Hey, how is …" She paused to look at his name tag. "How is Graham here supposed to give us his full opinion if he doesn't know all the details?"

I dropped my hand and looked at Graham. "Sorry for putting you on the spot."

Graham shrugged. "It breaks up the monotony. And I'd rather have something like this happen at one of my tables than have someone yell at me because their order was wrong."

"I'm glad my love life—or lack thereof—is here to amuse you," I told him.

Leslie leaned closer to Graham. "Sorry about my friend. She's crabby because she hasn't gotten laid in quite a while."

I rolled my eyes.

"Hey, I'm just saying, what kind of guy doesn't want to get laid?"

Graham rubbed his jaw. "He might have his reasons. Maybe he really likes you and wants to take it slow."

Leslie snorted. "They haven't even exchanged phone numbers. I think it's weird they've only been messaging through the dating app."

Graham lifted his chin. "Where's your phone?"

I pulled my cell from my purse. "Here."

"Pull up the app and send him a message. Ask him for his phone number. Tell him it's time you got more personal."

"I don't know," I said hesitantly.

Leslie snatched the phone from my hand and started tapping away.

I realized I could easily take it back but didn't bother. I was on my second glass of beer, so while I wasn't buzzed enough to drunk-text, I was loose enough to let my friend do it for me.

Graham moved behind Leslie and watched her type.

"How does that sound?" she asked him.

He nodded. "Good."

"And send," Leslie said and handed my phone back to me.

I quickly looked at what she'd written.

> Me: Hey. We've gone on three dates now, and I like you. What do you say we get off this dating app and you give me your phone number?

A second later, a message popped up.

> Joel: Why do you want my phone number?

I read the message out loud. I couldn't tell if he was flirting back or if he was being evasive.

Leslie snatched my phone back.

"What are you typing?" I asked.

She didn't answer. Instead, she typed away and handed it back.

> Me: How else am I supposed to call you and whisper dirty things in your ear?

I looked up at my best friend. "Really? I can't believe you sent that."

She shrugged and took a sip of her drink. "If he doesn't give it to you after that, he doesn't like you, or he's a serial killer."

Graham moved back in between us. "Serial killer?"

"Yeah," Leslie said in a *duh* tone. "He doesn't want his number traced back to him after he kills Indy."

"Thanks," I said.

She shrugged. "If the shoe fits ..."

Graham laughed. "You're weird. But this has been fun." He looked at me. "Good luck."

"Thanks."

Graham walked away, and my phone pinged.

Leslie rubbed her hands together. "Moment of truth."

> Joel: 651-555-3825

"He gave me his number," I said in surprise. I hadn't realized how much I'd thought he'd say no until then.

"Maybe he's not a serial killer after all," Leslie said.

I looked up from my phone. "That sounds very reassuring."

She shrugged. "That's what I'm here for."

———

Get My Wrong Number now!

ABOUT THE AUTHOR

R.L. Kenderson is two best friends writing under one name.

Renae has always loved reading, and in third grade, she wrote her first poem where she learned she might have a knack for this writing thing. Lara remembers sneaking her grandmother's Harlequin novels when she was probably too young to be reading them, and since then, she knew she wanted to write her own.

When they met in college, they bonded over their love of reading and the TV show *Charmed*. What really spiced up their friendship was when Lara introduced Renae to romance novels. When they discovered their first vampire romance, they knew there would always be a special place in their hearts for paranormal romance. After being unable to find certain storylines and characteristics they wanted to read about in the hundreds of books they consumed, they decided to write their own.

One lives in the Minneapolis-St. Paul area and the other in the Kansas City area where they both work in the medical field during the day and a sexy author by night. They communicate through phone, email, and whole lot of messaging.

You can find them at http://www.rlkenderson.com, Facebook, Instagram, TikTok, and Goodreads. Join their reader group! Or you can email them at rlkenderson@ rlkenderson.com, or sign up for their newsletter. They always love hearing from their readers.

Made in the USA
Coppell, TX
25 February 2024

29420349R00164